One Foot Outside The Door

Amorous Trilogy, Volume 1 Vina St. Fran

Published by Vina St. Fran, 2015.

One Foot Outside The Door

Amorous Trilogy, Volume 1

Vina St. Fran

Published by Vina St. Fran, 2015.

ONE FOOT OUTSIDE THE DOOR

First edition. April 15, 2015. Copyright © 2015 Vina St. Fran. ISBN: 978-0996139403

Written by Vina St. Fran.

FIRST PUBLISHED 2007 by ZAM Publishing, LLC.

32455 W. 12 Mile Road # 3346 Farmington Hills, MI 48333

One Foot Outside The Door: the Amorous Trilogy

Layout by Penoaks Publishing,

http://penoaks.com

Dedication

I dedicate this to the people who have been my rock throughout the years: my parents, my sibling, my extended family, my friends, and especially my son, Zachary. To my friends and family who have stuck by me through thick and thin, this book is for you. Your unending support, patience, and faith in me have been the driving force behind all that I've accomplished. A special shoutout to my college BFF, Dawn.

Look at us now!

My son, you have blossomed into a remarkable young man, full of drive and curiosity. Thanks to you, I have been reminded over and over again that it is important to follow one's dreams without fear. This dedication is a symbol of your undying devotion and the promising future ahead of you.

This dedication is for every writer who has ever dared to follow their passion and put pen to paper. Let us celebrate creativity, the art of storytelling, and the release that comes from crafting something truly remarkable out of words. This dedication is meant to remind us of the common ground we share in our love of literature and the infinite potential it holds for all of us.

Thank you for joining me on this literary journey, and best wishes to everyone who reads it. Your participation and encouragement will help these words come to life, inspiring thought and moving people. You add so much to the narrative, and these stories were written just for you.

I dedicate this work with profound gratitude and affection to my delightful mother, son, my family, my friends, and every writer who dares to dream. Let us keep encouraging one another and fostering a world where dreams are valued, fostered, and made real.

CHAPTER ONE

There are men who speak about their penis as if it is an extended member of their family. They damn near burst out of their pants to make the introduction. The thing they fail to realize is that, for most women, inches can't compensate for character or a man's worth.

Cyndarella Worthy's mama always told her how to behave like a lady throughout much of her life. Except when it came to the subject of men. Perhaps had they had such conversations, it would have spared Cyn the consequential heartache she racked up in dating deadbeats.

Hell, Cyn pouted, most women don't realize they're dating a fucking' loser until each layer is peeled back piece by piece like an onion. So much so, it ends up making everything around you tear.

First of all, you got to check off the outer layer. Of course he's dangerously fine, like Terrance Howard. All the way down to that little smirk of a smile on his face that initially drives you wild. This is a man that any mother would pray her daughter would bring home. A well groomed professional man with the material trimmings that would make most women's hearts swoon, and let's not neglect to mention that big fat bank account.

Accompanying this package are the big boy-toys, you know, the E-Class Mercedes Benz, and perhaps a Hummer or some other luxury SUV parked next to the Benz in his three-car garage. And, imagine, there is an empty spot waiting he's been saving just for you! He's a go-getter on the fast track career-wise. Heck, there ain't anything sexier than a man on a mission!

Three months have passed and by now you've discovered

the middle layer. Your potential Mr. Right is charming, blends into most social settings and loves to shower you with affection. And yes, you've hit the sheets with him to find he is equipped with a substantial-sized tool to drill you deep in the wee hours of the night.

Women lie when they say size don't matter, Cyn reasoned.

In her clinical experience, Cyn found fucking men with little dicks required much more work in order for her to achieve an orgasm. God forbid if they suffered from premature ejaculation! For her it wasn't an option she desired to explore.

Getting to the inner layer some six months later, you find that things aren't quite working out. Mr. Right has fast become Mr. Wrong. He starts calling you less and making excuses why he's unavailable. And when you are together, his cell phone rings all through the night, and he can't seem to keep his lies straight as to who's on the other end of the phone. It is then you realize the object of your affection has started to show his ass and, of course, it's all because he thinks things are moving way too fast. He needs time to sort things out. Bottom line is, Mr. Lover Man isn't ready to commit and has moved on to his next conquest.

Examining herself, at thirty-two, Cyn was striking in appearance. Yet, she was further from the altar than she'd ever been. Not only that, Cyn had what she called the five Bs: bank, beauty, boobs, booty and brains. And the fact she hadn't become a member of the single mothers' club made her stick her chest out even more. But wouldn't you know, some people viewed her as selfish because of this? That was their problem, not hers.

Thad Mitchell, Cyn's latest flame, was a bit different from the usual targets she dated. He was divorced with a four- year-old daughter. Normally, Cyn didn't do men with baby mommas because she hated the drama that went along with it. Too many of her girlfriends had suffered just because they made the mistake of falling in love with a man who had dependents. Despite their good intentions, some men never truly, completely made a clean break.

It just so happened Cyn lucked out, because Thad's ex got remarried overseas to a fellow naval officer, so Thad rarely got weekend visits. It was more of a long- distance phone relationship. Heather, his ex, was great about sending family videos and photos. Thad visited twice a year, which Cyn encouraged because she sure as hell didn't want anything getting in the middle of quality time with her man, namely him drowning his sorrows because he missed his little girl.

At eight months old, the relationship was still quite fresh and Thad agreed to something most men couldn't seem to follow through on: courtship. That was the one stipulation Cyn had before she'd accept a single date with a man. And if he wasn't consistent, forget about it! Three months into their courtship, Thad hadn't failed her. With a demanding high profile career, Cyn rarely had time for anything more than an occasional fling every now and then. Not that she minded variety at all, but she had to admit, her favorite slogan, 'A few good men', was starting to get stale.

Thad was eye candy at its finest. At 6' 5", weighing in around 280 pounds, his body was definitely lean and mean. He had fair skin and a strong jaw line, accompanied by keen facial features that appeared like they had been chiseled into place. The thought alone of staring up into Thad's piercing hazel eyes made her ache to be with him. And being with him felt right. She was satisfied with the way they were progressing. She kept her fingers crossed that they would stay that way.

CHAPTER TWO

Cyn considered herself a Detroiter, even though she didn't reside in the city. In most places, that didn't matter, but in Detroit, to some Black folks, it did. Detroit's dirty little secret of being one of the most segregated cities in America had recently been exposed. But it was nothing new to Cyndarella, who'd experienced it firsthand. The attitude was if you were Black, you had to live on the Detroit side of Eight Mile, and if you didn't, you were a sellout. Many Black-owned businesses in the city had rejected to work with Cyn initially because her office wasn't in the (313) area code. Racism on any level disturbed Cyn, but it was especially disappointing when it was within the Black community.

Slavery had been abolished well over one hundred years, and yet the mental shackles and attitudes kept some enslaved. People were still burning crosses on lawns of neighbors with skin complexions other than White, and recently in Livonia, a middle class suburb, angry residents had been very vocal about opposing a new twenty-four-hour Wal-Mart in their neighborhood. Some were actually quoted as saying Black people would bring more crime in their town if Wal-Mart moved into their backyard, stunning Cyn as well as local politicians. But it really shouldn't have, seeing Livonia was named as the Whitest city in America. That wasn't a bad thing; it was the attitude of several but not most of the residents who lived there.

Detroit, like most urban cities, had problems. They needed to find a solution and in some areas they had. Downtown Detroit was one of the safest areas in the country. Hart Plaza also hosted large ethnic festivals throughout the summer, free of charge. During the winter, families could go down to Campus Martius with their families to ice skate. The Motown Winter Blast was also a delight with two years under its belt. There was a giant slide made of snow, as well as live entertainment. And this year it was amazing because of the Super Bowl. The positive feedback from visiting tourists gave Detroit a much-needed boost in the eyes of Americans. The downside was, most Detroiters couldn't afford to go to the Super Bowl, or the A-list parties, and they were in their own backyard.

Last year's mayoral race had been closely watched throughout the country. Kwame Kilpatrick, the city's youngest mayor, was fighting to save his job. He admitted he'd made some mistakes, and the media made sure that everybody knew about it. Part of his campaign message was to give him another chance as mayor. Freeman Hendrix, his opponent, came close to taking that right away from Kwame, but in the end, the residents chose to re-elect him. But it was apparent that, by the narrow margin between the mayor and his challenger, Freeman Hendrix, the citizens were not going to be so openhanded with their vote next time.

One area that seemed to be neglected during the campaigning was the fact that forty-seven per cent of Detroiters were illiterate. How would the Kilpatrick administration address that? It remained to be seen. For her part, Cyn volunteered with a number of homeless shelters and food banks in the area to do whatever she could to give back to those less fortunate than herself.

Scrutiny was nothing new for Cyn. She took pride in how she carried herself and it showed in her demeanor. She pronounced her words articulately, to the chagrin of some observers. She heard the rumors people spread about her, saying that she was trying to be White, just because of how she talked. Sometimes she fucked with them on purpose because she knew they would talk shit about her. It was known that Cyndarella had dated men of all backgrounds. Tongues had wagged over it. Speculation further provoked skepticism about her character because of how she'd left her former career in radio behind. She'd told her asshole of a manager to go fuck himself in the main lobby of the radio station and stormed off to start a business of her own.

Oh yeah, Cyn heard the rumors, but that was all they were. Earning frequent fucking miles on her back was not the way she did business. The confidence she exuded, from tossing her hair to the way her hips swayed when she walked, ignited jealousy among her female peers in social circles, but Cyn didn't dare to try to befriend them. She had friends. Not to mention the accounts she managed to land. Time had proven the naysayers wrong, because Peachtree had blossomed into a successful agency without her using her body.

Cyn was CEO of Peachtree Productions, an advertising agency she'd started at the ripe old age of twenty-five, specializing in minority brand marketing and advertising campaigns. Cyn had established a nice reputation for herself in the past seven years, managing to retain local automobile dealerships, retailers and other accounts. She'd found her career extremely time-consuming but rewarding.

She enjoyed creating savvy marketing campaigns for her clients, especially when she tracked their return on investment. In some cases, especially with auto dealerships, Cyn helped them move more than half of their inventory in record time. Needless to say, looking out for her clients' bottom line increased hers as well.

CHAPTER THREE

Rummaging through her clustered walk- in closet in search of something to wear was a task Cyn dreaded. Tonight was special to her. It was Girl's Night Out, a monthly ritual she shared with her three childhood friends, Corvette, Denise and Tavie. It was their time to catch up. Frantically looking through the closet for something to wear was always a challenge and the last thing Cyn needed was another interruption, but try telling that to the caller on the other end of the ringing phone.

"Hello".

"Hey, girl, it's Tavie. What's up?" "My dress." "Ha, ha, ha, you're funny as hell."

"I was trying to decide what to wear tonight and I can't decide on shit."

"Cyn, don't make me come through this phone and shake you. With all those clothes you got hanging in your closet, you know you're full of shit."

"Thanks for your vote of confidence! It's hard trying to look good all the time."

"Girl, you never change, I'll see you later on tonight!"

"Tav, hey, don't hang up. What's going on with you? I know we probably won't get a chance to talk much tonight one on one."

"Girl, I'm just tired of Mack's dumb ass. That ex of his called me again, this time while I was on my job and I cannot believe she would take it there. Shit, it's been three years, girl! When will she learn? Hey, Cyn, got to grab my other line. See ya later."

With that, Octavia Slade, a beautiful, petite pecancomplexioned sister, was gone. Cyn knew something was wrong. She heard it in Tavie's voice and it was a Mack mess as usual. Mackenzie Dooley was a principal in the same school district of Southfield where Tav was a third grade elementary teacher. They'd met at a district meeting almost three years ago and they'd been inseparable ever since. Problem was Mack had the Clinton disease: women. Single and divorced mothers adored him. The teacher and faculty openly competed like crazy for this man's attention, and Mack made sure Tavie knew it.

Mack wasn't Cyn's type. He actually reminded her of a mature-looking Urkel on *Family Matters*. The only difference was he sported a beard and mustache. Mack came from a close-knit wealthy family in the affluent community of Bloomfield Hills. He was the youngest and his mother still treated him as if he were in diapers. Not only that, Mom was always trying to introduce Mack to other women behind Tavie's back. Knowing this, Tavie continued to kiss up to her, but Cyn wouldn't dare play that stupid. She'd confront the bitch. Mack said Tavie should lighten up and joked about it, which tickled Mrs. Dooley to death. For an old broad, Mrs. D looked great. Cyn hoped to look that good when she reached her sixties. Cyn tried not to mind her friend's business, but now this was taking a toll on Tavie, it didn't sit well with her one bit.

The Slade family had moved into a house across the street from Cyn's family while in junior high school. They'd met at the annual block party one summer and became fast friends. Throughout college, the girls had remained close, despite the fact they went to different universities. Tavie attended Southern University in Baton Rouge, while Cyn went to Eastern Michigan University in Ypsilanti.

Tavie completed her undergraduate studies and got engaged to Tyrone Sutton, defensive lineman for the New Orleans Saints, but later found out he was having an affair with a high-priced call girl. A photographer spotted them making out on Canal Street in the French Quarter and plastered the revealing pictures on the cover of every newspaper in town. The local news couldn't stop vomiting up the scandal, causing Tavie to escape New Orleans in humiliation. Later Tavie came back to Detroit and completed her graduate studies at Wayne State University, though she remained bitter for a long time.

CHAPTER FOUR

There were tons of cars parked at Jazzman's Supper Club tonight and Cyn knew it was going to be quite an evening. It was 7:30 P.M. and the place was jumping. Anybody who wanted to be seen frequented Jazzman's on the weekends. Pulling up in her Millennium Infiniti QX4 Gold SUV, Cyn waited patiently for the valet attendant to wait on her. "Ms. Worthy, don't you look beautiful as usual," Jorge the Valet attendant greeted Cyn with his thick Mexican accent. "Thank you, Jorge."

""Believe me, it's my pleasure. Enjoy your evening," Jorge said, handing her a ticket.

Sightseeing definitely took on a new meeting tonight at Jazzman's. Singles and couples dressed to impress. Jazzman's was legendary for famous smiles and faces.

"What a nice fur. Can I check it for you?" Cyn heard a familiar young woman ask. She removed her mink and handed it to Maxine, who was checking the coat out a little too much for Cyn's liking but she didn't want to cause a scene by going into bitch mode.

"Ms. Cyn, how's Pete?"

"Peter and his wife are doing just fine, Max." Cyn caught a quick flicker of sadness in Max's eyes and, for a moment, she looked away.

Trying to take her mind off the moment, Cyn decided to compliment the woman on her appearance. Definitely a plus-size sister, maybe a size 16 on a good day, she looked really cute in her little tuxedo-hostess ensemble. Besides, tonight she was definitely making Fashion Fair proud with her Tawny Glo foundation and Raisin Wine lipstick.

"You look good, Max. I know Pete is my brother, but he is a dick.

You're lucky God didn't stop making men when he made Pete".

"Cyn, it isn't a secret how you feel about me and Pete. Married or not, the man knows how to handle his business, if you know what I mean?" Max asserted, while handing Cyn a claim ticket. "Some of us women are happy to take what we can get!"

Disgusted Cyn walked away before she cussed the ignorant plump woman out. The fact her older brother was a complete dog didn't make her feel good. Pete had a wonderful wife at home, and that's where he chose to leave her most of the time when he came back for a visit.

Lively conversation and laughter roared out from the section where the ladies shared dinner and cocktails, with the exception of a very tardy Tavie. Denise Lincoln was the most stable in terms of a committed marital relationship. And she was truly a beautiful person inside and out. Denise's bright red hair and freckles made her stand out—a fact Dee hated. She was employed at Peachtree as the Creative Director, where she worked her tail off. And Cyn compensated her very well financially.

"Ladies, ready for another round for the table?" their waiter, Orville, cooed.

"Another round of what, Orville?" Corvette taunted back. Corvette Vern, a wannabe blond bombshell was the one and only White girl of the group.

"Orville, start us on our first round, please," Cyn requested.

"Grey Goose vodka martini, shaken, not stirred, with lots of bleu cheese and stuffed olives, right, for you, my lady? And two green apple martinis coming up," Orville chirped.

"You're awesome!" Cyn exclaimed to Orville before he ran

off to place their order.

Intimate, the house jazz band, was jamming as usual. Right now they were covering Boney James' CD, *Boneyism*—

and even Boney would have been bobbing his head in appreciation. "So, ladies, I've got some serious gossip. Do I start now, or do you

want to wait for Tavie?"

"Vette, who or what is it about this time, huh?" Denise queried. "Whatever the fuck it is about, I know y'all asses better wait on

me!" Tavie spat out upon her entrance, forcing everyone to move over and create room for her in the booth. As usual, Tavie's hair was laid.

"Okay, so what did I miss?" Tavie asked.

"Well, Vette was about to give us some of the latest gossip," Denise replied.

"Vette, bring it on," Cyn encouraged. But before Vette could answer, Orville arrived with the first round of drinks.

"Lovely Tavie, I saw you come in. Please tell me you're having your favorite this evening, Long Island Iced Tea?"

"Damn, Orville, you're good. Yes, please a Long Island. Pronto."

"Here you are, gorgeous. I took the pleasure of ordering it when I noticed you'd arrived. I aim to please," Orville whispered into Tavie's ear.

"Orville, careful, darling. I love a man who aims to please!" Tavie flirted.

"Hold on now, lovely one, don't start something you can't finish," Orville challenged. Between the flirting, Orville managed to take the dinner order, and that gave the women a chance to catch up.

"Orville wants you, Tavie, but that flirting shit has got to wait. All right, Vette, spill all you know," Cyn urged.

Vette had started her own court-reporting business, which she ran out of her house. Ironically enough, the court was often the place she got her news.

"First, remember Tavie's ex-boyfriend, Lee Glover? Well, Lee is now a poppa of twin biracial girls," Vette tattled, while the women shook their heads in amazement at the news. Vette proceeded on as her friends listened in attentively.

"Check this out. Lee wanted a paternity test to prove he wasn't the father. Blood tests came back ninety-nine-point- five per cent that he's the baby's daddy. Gotcha!"

"Yeah, I see why now the motherfucker didn't want kids or marriage. He and Tyrone have a lot in common. They like to get their freak on with trash. He even claimed he only dated sisters!" Tavie blurted out with a shudder.

"You're lying! See, it's that shit right there that makes me hate men.

I hope you used rubbers!" Vette contended.

"He's gotta pay up. Obviously, when Lee was in heat, his black ass didn't package his meat." Denise quipped.

"I know there's more. What else?" Cyn questioned.

"There's more. Speaking of old flames, or maybe I should say, first loves." Cyn winced because she sure didn't want to think of her first love. It hurt too much to bear, even now. For a moment the table became quiet. The women bonded over a private moment as none cared to go back to that unspoken, yet unforgettable place in their lives.

CHAPTER FIVE

Orville was right on with his timing, delivering an array of delightful cuisine that danced on their taste buds. Somehow, Cyn's appetite seemed to fade before she could take a bite.

"Cyn, you are not going to believe this. I was doing a deposition at court last week for the Sadiq case and Bashar's name came up in the report. I couldn't help it, but when I got a moment, I asked Mr. Sadiq about Bashar, and he said Bashar was back here in the U.S. He wouldn't disclose more detail than that. Although he did say Bashar has been back for a while."

"I really don't care about Bashar or his whereabouts. Besides, we were babies back in high school. I'm way over it now!" Cyn protested.

"High school and college, you had your own Mid-Eastern prince, girlfriend," Vette joked, though it was apparent Cyndarella was not amused.

"Vette, do me a favor. If you could be so kind, please don't ask Mr. Sadiq any more questions about Bashar. It's ancient history now. Let it go. I appreciate you looking out for me, but don't dredge this up again."

"Okay Cyn. Don't worry, I got your back!" Vette countered. "No more gossip, because I want to keep my dessert down."

Tavie asserted.

"Okay, Tavie, did you fire your dry cleaner?" Cyn finally asked. "What's with the wrinkles?"

"I took a quick nap after I got dressed. Damn, I didn't even notice it. Mack should've told me."

"Tavie, do you think he is still messing around?" Denise inquired.

But almost before she could finish, Vette jumped in.

"Hell yeah, you know he's cheating. I saw him with some Vanity look-alike with braids at Beale Street restaurant, in downtown Pontiac at a happy hour last Friday."

"Wait a minute, why didn't you call me, Vette? We're supposed to look out for each other, remember?" Tavie could barely get the words out.

"I did try calling you and you didn't return my calls or texts. Mack didn't see me, and believe *me* they looked quite cozy. The chick wasn't hard on the eyes. She seemed to be a regular with the wait staff."

Reaching in her purse for her cell phone, Tavie started dialing. There was nothing like a game of Pistons basketball and tonight they were beating the hell out of Chicago, which was a good thing as far as Mack was concerned. It was half time and the pizza had finally arrived when Mack heard the phone ring. Looking at the caller ID, Mack answered.

"Hey, baby. Having a good time?"

"I was until I heard about you and some bitch with braids at Beale Street."

"Woman, I let you out of the house and you call me up with some bullshit? André wanted us to meet his new lady friend. Remember that, Tavie? Answer me!" Mack demanded.

"Yeah, I remember".

"I met them for drinks, and you didn't show because you had cramps."

"Let me make sure I have this right. Dre was with the woman

with braids? Mack, please don't lie to me. You promised!"

"Don't tell me what I promised, Tavie, it's getting old. No, Dre's woman doesn't wear braids. Her sister does and she is engaged. Look, my pizza is getting cold. Hurry home, baby. Love you." With that, Mack hung up before she could retort.

"Damn, who had she been talking to this time?" Mack wondered. He knew that it'd been a close call but he'd covered himself, and when Tavie got home he'd give her some loving so tough, her head would spin. It was going to be a good night.

"What did he say? What's his excuse this time?" Denise asked.

"He covered himself, that's all. Claims she's his boy's girlfriend's engaged sister. He thinks I believe him. I just finished cussing his ex out for calling and harassing me at work, and now this. Sorry, y'all, gotta go."

"Tav, don't tell him I told you because he already hates me. Keep it between us, okay?"

"I won't, don't worry, Vette. I'll call y'all soon."

"Can you believe that shit, he's got her snowed," Denise said with disgust, after Tavie stormed away.

"That skank didn't have a ring on her finger; she ain't engaged, y'all.

I'm willing to bet on that."

"It nauseates me like crazy that she stays with the son of a bitch. But that's on her," Cyn verbalized.

"Wait, though, you know the ole girl is going to give him some.

Mack's going to get into the panties tonight," Dee laughed.

"That's a damn shame!" Vette agreed.

"Ladies, enough of Mack and Tavie. I'm skipping dessert tonight; my honey is coming home after two long weeks. I need him in the worst way."

"Thad, Thad, Thad, he is fine, you got a keeper this time, Cyn Worthy." She could hear the admiration ringing from Denise's voice.

"I'm in total agreement with you." Cyn gently gave each woman a hug and left for the evening.

Denise watched as Cyn stepped away. She knew her friend was lying. Thad wasn't due to come in until Sunday, because Cyn had already reminded her she would be working from her home office Monday morning. The mention of Bashar had sent Cyn out into the night.

Aaliyah's song, *Rock the Boat*, blared from the stereo. The single was once a favorite of Cyn's, but tonight she was too distracted to notice it.

"Oh, what a night!" Cyn exclaimed out loud to herself, when her cell phone started ringing, interrupting her train of thought. She knew by the ring tone who was on the other end of her line.

"Yes, Denise".

"Don't yes Dee me, missy. Uh, Thad comes in on Sunday.

Why did you leave with that tired-ass excuse?"

Cyn couldn't help chuckling at her friend; she knew she was guilty as charged.

"Yeah, it was lame, but no one knew but you, and I hope you kept it to yourself."

"You know I did. Besides, I just wanted to check to see if you were okay."

"I'm stuffed, I ate like a pig. I'm taking my ass to bed after I've had a bath. We had a long week."

"Cyn, you threw down the appetizers, but you barely touched your dinner once Vette mentioned the dreaded 'B' word—and you know what I'm talking about!" Denise gently spoke to her friend.

"There might be some truth to that, but it's almost one and I'm not staying on the phone a minute longer. Enjoy the weekend, Dee, goodnight." With that, Cyn hung up before Denise could reply.

Shaker Heights Villa in Auburn Hills was the gated condominium complex Cyn called home. Being drunk with sleep didn't stop her from drawing a bath in her jetted bathtub. Silence wasn't always a bad thing. And right now, it was much needed.

CHAPTER SIX

"Baby, oh God, baby!" The warmth of a man's breath gently caressed Cyn's neck. "I love you." Her body was on fire and his dick was the only extinguisher that could put out the flames.

"I don't give a fuck about love, motherfucker," Cyn said to him as he entered her hot canal with force. "Just fuck me, please fuck me".

"Umm, you're so wet".

At this point, Cyn's taut nipples became his next target, as the man greedily sucked her twin peaks, causing her pussy to contract more tightly around his thick, enlarged cock. Both of them started to sweat more profusely as they wildly gave in to passion.

"Come, Cyn!"

"No! Not yet".

"Come on, bitch, stop holding back, you know you love this dick, don't you? Don't you?" Bashar was yelling.

With her legs wrapped tightly around his broad shoulders, Bashar forcefully entered her while grabbing her ass and delving deeper into her soul. Cyn was addicted to the intensity of their lovemaking and the heights they seemed to reach.

"It feels so good to be with you like this again, Bashar, it's been too long."

At this very moment, the chime of the alarm clock went off. It had been years since Cyn had thought of Bashar, and yet the ferocity of her dream reminded her that, despite the years gone by, she still hadn't forgotten him. "Damn it!" she cursed. "Damn you, Vette!" she muttered under her breath. Why did Vette have to bring him back up?

CHAPTER SEVEN

Cyn refused to even speak the name, Bashar Bazzi. He was her former high school and college sweetheart. They'd met while attending classes at Southfield-Lathrup High School, where Cyn had been a cheerleader for the basketball team and Bashar a point guard. Cyn grew up in Southfield, a diverse upper middle class suburb outside of Detroit. The neighborhood encompassed a proud mixed heritage of African-American, Jewish and Chaldean residents. As a matter of fact, Southfield had won a Spirit of Michigan Award for Diversity, given by the state of Michigan, five years in a row.

The subdivisions in the neighborhood were filled with kids from various ethnic backgrounds. Looking back, Cyn viewed it as an advantage because she'd become knowledgeable about the racial and religious backgrounds of the families in the neighborhood. For one, the Southfield Public School System observed the Jewish holiday. The teachers provided an educational account of what the somberness of Yom Kippur symbolized, as well as the celebrations of Rosh Hashanah and Hanukkah, which bridged the gap between the students. It was really like an open forum because they addressed just about any issue that arose. Cyn was convinced that her upbringing in Southfield had helped her become the dynamic woman that she was today.

Cyn recalled her first encounter with Bashar during her sophomore year at Southfield High. After cheerleading practice, Denise, Tavie and Vette had decided to hang out and watch the basketball players practice their hoops. The girls were cheerleaders and had already dated a few of the players, though Cyn hadn't bothered; she preferred college guys.

"Hey, look at Sean, he's fine as hell," Denise screamed out

loud. "Yeah, and he got a serious game," Tavie sallied back in agreement.

Vette wandered over to her man on the team, Mark Olson, a biracial brother whom Vette had been slam-dunking with occasionally on and off. From the looks of it now, they were definitely on. Tavie and Denise followed suit soon, leaving Cyn to watch alone. That's when the basketball, thrown out of bounds, hit her on her thigh.

"Sorry, sexy."

"Don't be, just don't let it happen again," Cyn said sarcastically. "Or what will you do?" That's when they locked eyes for the first time and it was thrilling. Cyn checked out the handsome Chaldean wannabe Michael Jordan and she had to admit she liked what she saw. While watching him practice, she hadn't helped but notice he had rhythm.

"I won't be as nice as I am now, that's for sure."

"Ooh, you promise! C'mon, you know you dig me, Cyn. I saw you checking me out."

"Obviously, you know my name. What's yours?" Cyn asked. "Bashar, baby."

"Let's get something straight. I'm not your baby! If I dig you, make no mistake about it, you'll know it." With that, Cyn walked away with Bashar staring after her, his mouth open.

"Damn, I was crazy to think it would last forever," Cyn sighed out loud to herself, as she trotted over to her bathroom and slipped out of her silk chemise gown. She looked admiringly at herself naked in the mirror.

"Not bad, girl," she winked to herself, although she knew perfectly well she had to work at keeping everything in place. Not one to brag, Cyn considered herself to be strikingly attractive, even beautiful, whenever she went the extra mile, which was more often than she cared to admit. While grabbing a towel from the linen closet, she smelled the aroma of Jamaica Blue Mountain coffee in the air. "Thank heavens for my trusted friend, Mr. Coffee!" she exclaimed.

Climbing into the shower, she heard the weatherman's forecast of mostly mid-twenties temperatures for the weekend. Lathering up with one of her favorite refreshing body scrubs by Origins made her awfully giddy, despite the fact that, ten minutes earlier, she'd dreaded starting the day. Nothing was better than a morning shower—except sex. No, a correction:

good sex. Which, by the way, she would not have access to until tomorrow when Thad came home.

CHAPTER EIGHT

Speaking of Thad, Cyn blushed when she thought of the messages her man had left on her voicemail last night. It was enough to make her want to be a graduating senior in the class of masturbation, but she always failed with her attempts. God, she missed Thad. He was a senior internal auditor for Daimler Chrysler in Auburn Hills. He had been in Singapore for the last two weeks, and now he was on a plane headed home. Pouring herself a cup of coffee, she still found it hard to believe she was enjoying such a healthy relationship with him.

At the beginning, Cyn had been reluctant to have a monogamous relationship because she did not trust men. Period! She found the more she tried to give them a chance, the more they let her down, every damn time! They seemed to be busy playing women like checker pieces on a board, or maybe she just wasn't ready at the time. Having a man for Cyn meant he was an enhancement, not a necessity, a fact she blatantly shared with would-be suitors. Always upfront, she warned Thad he would have to earn her trust. And she gave him a probationary period to boot, which he passed!

Cyn was pleased. She had a relationship that wasn't toxic and with a brother. She'd dated her share of men, being the connoisseur that she was. Men were men; fuck what folks said about the race, it was a bunch of nonsense! White men fucked up just as bad as Black men did. Cyn didn't take shit from any of them. Cyn's mother constantly ranted to her daughter that she was not a queen for a day, she ruled forever, and if a man couldn't respect her he had to go.

The conversations often took place after the fact. Yeah, she listened to her mother, but she screwed up along the way, too.

She turned up her nose in disgust at the relationship woes that seemed to summon her for duty. She'd met a lot of charity cases along the way. In her early twenties, she'd figured the bigger the dick and the stronger the lick of the clit, then satisfaction was guaranteed in all areas of life; nothing else seemed to matter.

Thinking back on those days made Cyn a bit remorseful over precious time she'd wasted. But back than, her only interest had been getting laid and paid. The latter she managed on her own, for she would never allow a man to provide anything to her financially, other than gifts. It amazed her how some of today's women asked men for money to pay their bills in exchange for sex, and yet they were offended to be called prostitutes. The only man that could pay her bills would be her husband.

Cyn and Bashar had lived together briefly during college. Bashar mapped out their future: they'd finish college first and then marry. Afterwards, they'd start a business together. Bashar supported them working at his father's liquor store, but he was determined for them to have a life autonomous of his family. Bashar's plan worked so well until the day his father confronted Cyn before she left for class. Mr. Bazzi informed her that Bashar would be leaving to go to Baghdad on business and he didn't want Cyn to influence his son otherwise. Mr. Bazzi informed Cyn he could not make the trip because of his health, so he was sending his sons in his place.

Cyn would never forget how emphatic Mr. Bazzi was in telling her family obligations came first. She listened, but the bottom line was that, even after four years, Bashar's family still hadn't accepted her. Common sense revealed that much. She was tolerated but not accepted, and she was crushed. The fact Bashar left a week after New Year's Day in 1991 didn't help matters, to say the least. He could do little to console her before he left for Baghdad. He went, never return again and it shattered everything she dared to believe about love and trust. It wasn't like she didn't try to play the waiting game; she did, but lost. From that moment on, Cyn promised herself, hell would freeze over before she'd ever let a man fuck her over again.

CHAPTER NINE

Tonight had been a good time with the girls, except when Vette had mentioned Bashar and the bitch with braids. Cyn had looked like a deer caught in the headlights when Vette said that Bashar was back in the States. That motherfucker had left her, and that was not to mention his follow-up skills, which he lacked big time. Bashar didn't bother writing or calling Cyn whom he claimed he'd loved for four years. Tavie had to admit they'd been the couple to watch for, because of their intense commitment to each other. Hell, they'd seemed solid, Tavie guessed, but not to the Bazzi family.

The one thing that ticked Tavie off was how the Muslims and Chaldeans brought their asses over to the good old United States and got over on operating gas stations and party stores. There was not a main street in Detroit that was exempt from the liquor stores that seemed to pop up on every corner. And if you wanted to know the thanks Black people got for spending their hard-earned dollars and food stamps? Hiked-up prices and bad treatment in urban areas. It was prevalent in some of the poorest neighborhoods. Several news stations went undercover and reported that, in certain stores, the groceries weren't fresh and the owners were caught on camera saying they'd take care of it. When the camera crews went back in, they busted them again for the same problem. Competing Chaldean and Muslim grocery stores within the area that actually had fresh meat and produce saw an increase of traffic. Not to mention the personalized service which customers got. Most employees of the stores were on a first name basis with their regulars.

Like a moth to a flame, Middle Eastern men were drawn to women of color. But they acted like they thought their own women were too good for any other race except them. That didn't stop them from always trying to get pussy from a sister. Cyn wasn't the only one who'd gotten some dick from them; Tavie'd had too and it was good. Geographically, the Middle East wasn't too far from the coast of Africa, so maybe that had something to do with them having big dicks. At least the ones Tavie'd fucked. There was a lot of stereotyping within interracial relationships, Tavie thought. Black men knew how to find the most unattractive White woman, and just because she happened to be White, they'd kiss her ass and treat her like a goddess. Some of the brothers wouldn't even look a sister's way. If you were Black, get back, and if you were White, you were all right, in their textbook. Some of her Black male peers felt this way. She asked them how they could choose a woman based on race and not with their heart, and they told her they were more attracted to Caucasian women because they were easier to get along with. Black women, on the other hand, had a bad attitude. She asked one, "Your mother is Black! Does she have a bad attitude?"

If you polled a group of black women and asked them what kind of man were they looking for, they'd be quick to point out a *Black* man. These same women were often sitting at home on a Saturday night by themselves, making it a Blockbuster movie night. Tavie wasn't exempt from thinking along these lines, but she had become more realistic. If she hadn't found love with Mack, she would have been open to dating men from every background. She had been before she started dating him.

The recent talk around town about brothers being on the down-low scared Tavie. These men were spreading HIV to unsuspecting, trusting female partners. People had a right to their sexual orientation whether they were open or in the closet. Personally, she felt sexuality didn't define who you were. When all was said and done, you were going to be remembered for who you were as a human being, not for what you did in the bedroom. Tavie cared that this concrete issue plaguing the Black community was taking away lives. Black women had to take this into consideration. Hopefully, they would keep an open mind in exploring the playing field. The brothers definitely were.

White men had different expectations when it came to dating Black women. Most sisters had to be educated and professional, not to mention absolutely gorgeous. They had to make sure the woman was something of a conversation piece so their families would accept them. In rare occurrences, some White men were too cowardly to take a woman home to meet their families. And why was this? Unfortunately, it was due to the color of her face.

Tavie wasn't attracted to most White men unless they were soap-opera-fine, like the actors on daytime television. There were a couple of hotties that caught her attention. The actor who portrayed Dusty Donavan on *As the World Turns* was fine as hell. And he dated a sister for a couple of years in his personal life. Of course, her biggest crush was for the character, Deacon Sharp, on *The Bold and the Beautiful*. Man, if she could have a night with him...well, she did, sort of. Tavie set her TIVO daily so that she could check him out

CHAPTER TEN

Tavie sure wished she hadn't stopped smoking, because right now she could use a Capri. She and Mack shared a condo in Cumberland Village in Southfield, where she had been sitting out in the garage for the last ten minutes wondering who the latest conquest was for Mack this time. He'd tried hard to cover himself earlier, but female intuition never lied. Either that, or it was her PMS, which had been flaring up more since she'd started taking that new birth control pill, Yasmin.

If she weren't so tired, she would have driven up to Okemos to visit with her parents instead of coming home. Mustering the mental strength left in her, she closed the garage door and got out of her Expedition. Stalling for time, she fumbled around for her keys when Mack opened the door for her and took her in his arms.

"Hey, baby. The Pistons lost again. Chauncey was smoking. He got thirty-one points, and the rest of those chumps didn't do shit."

"That is fucked up. What you watching now?"

"*Nip/Tuck*, and woman, you know every time I watch that show, it gets me horny."

Tavie was quiet, and Mack sensed that she wasn't in a playful mood, so he decided he'd follow her lead and not come on too strong. She made a beeline for the bedroom as she didn't want to get into another argument with him

"I'll join you after I take a shower. It's been a long day," she said tersely.

"Whatever you say, baby."

Tavie deliberately discarded her clothes, leaving a trail on the living room floor as she walked away, and Mack stared after her.

Purposely locking the door, she turned on the stereo they had in the bathroom and popped in Mariah Carey's latest CD. She loved the way they had remodeled the bathroom with rich warm tones. It was one of her favorite places in the house. Reaching for towels out of the linen closet, she wasn't surprised when she heard Mack trying to pry open the door. She turned on the shower as he walked away. She put her shower cap on and hopped in, and it felt good having warm water all over her body.

Mack decided to chill a bottle of Tattinger Champagne and have it waiting, after Tavie had almost busted him earlier. It was her favorite. Smelling the steam from her shower, mixed in with a little of the Prescriptives body gel she liked, turned Mack on in a big way. Heading for their bedroom with the champagne and flutes, he sprawled out on the bed in his silk pajama bottoms which he favored and tried to act like he was watching *Nip/Tuck* while waiting for Tavie to come out of the bathroom. Mack loved anything silky rubbed up against his body. The slight friction gave him an instant hard-on.

Tavie applied an oil-free moisturizer to her face and quickly ran her fingers through her short hair. Right now, she really wanted to escape her man, but she had no place to run to because they lived together. She loved Mack but it was difficult trusting him. She knew she couldn't stay holed up in the bathroom. She finished up and went to join up with a waiting Mackenzie.

"Damn, Tav, I thank Halle Berry for bringing short hair back in style. You look beautiful, baby."

"Thanks, you don't look so bad yourself. Mmm, champagne. What's the special occasion?"

"See, Tavie, that's messed everything up, you asking me junk like that. All of a sudden it has to be an occasion to sip champagne

37

with my woman—"

Tavie cut him off before he could speak. "Look, Mack don't start no arguments with me tonight. I'm not questioning your defensive ass, you got that? I hope you realize it makes you look guilty," she whined in her favorite little girl voice that she used to annoy him.

"Okay, Tav, let me finish what I was saying, 'cause tonight you really need to hear this."

Tavie started nervously pacing when Mack got off the bed and went to her.

"I've fucked up in the past, but we hung in there and we're still together. There isn't nothing out there I couldn't have if I wanted it, but being with you has changed that."

Tavie couldn't believe her ears. Was Mack trying to ask her to marry him? Seeing the confused look on her face, Mack clarified his statement.

"What I meant to say is, this isn't time for me to get on my knees and start proposing on the spot. But I will as soon as the time is right."

With that, Tavie began to melt and, once again, Mack was given the benefit of the doubt. This time it was different. It *had* to be! How could she not trust him or get behind his declaration? The man even had tears in his eyes because he was overcome with love for her! She'd never seen this side of him, so vulnerable. They hugged between kisses, and once again, she told him she felt their relationship was secure.

"Now, that's what I'm talking about, baby. I hate it when you're so negative about our relationship and everything. Here, have some champagne." Mack handed her a flute, as he lay stretched out on their bed. Something about champagne made Tavie hot. Not that she wasn't anyway, but it made her a bit more daring and, damn, Mack liked seeing the wild side of his woman.

"Wait, let me fix this." Tavie laid her face in Mack's lap, feeling his engorged member against her cheek. Feeling the hardness of his dick intoxicated her even more than she already was. Aggressively, she gave him a blowjob that made his toes curl.

Mack positioned her round brown ass in his face and they began to sixty-nine each other. He snaked his tongue in and out of her pussy, tasting the tartness of her nectar. The more he licked the wetter she got. Mack was on the verge on coming but he decided he wasn't going out like that. He was making love to Tavie tonight. They both needed it.

"Mack, ooh, now! Hurry!"

"Yeah, Boo, but I want to love you tonight, alright?" "That's an offer I can't refuse."

Mounting Tavie, Mack held her close as he entered her. The warmth of her pussy propelled him to drive more and more deeply inside her. She was his, there was no question about it, and he wanted to make sure she knew it. From her response she was almost there.

"Tav, whose pussy is this? Huh, huh?" Mack shouted. "Yours, only yours, Mack. Always, I swear!"

"Promise me, it's only mine, Tavie." Looking at the sincerity of emotion in her face brought him to the point of no return before she could respond.

"Baby, I'm coming, okay?"

"It's your pussy, c'mon, big fella." With that Mack unloaded inside Tavie and collapsed upon her, bodies damp with their sweat.

"I love you Mack", she said kissing him on his lips.

"Love you, too." Mack felt more connected to Tavie tonight than he had in a long time. If he could be sure it would always be like this, he'd marry her right now.

Holding one another, Tavie closed her eyes while

Mack drifted off to sleep. Yeah, tonight Mack had proved his love for her, but the thing she despised was being lied to and, for sure, she knew she'd better not hear about him hanging out with some skank-assed bitch again. And God help him if she was sporting braids!

CHAPTER ELEVEN

Denise sure was glad the weekend had arrived. Waking up, she stretched and yawned. Looking at the clock, she screamed. It was almost 11 o'clock and she had missed her hair appointment! But she wasn't even having that. Her hair was nappy and she needed a touch up. Linda would have to let her come in. Pressing the speed dial button on her phone, Dee called the salon to reschedule her appointment for later.

"Linda's Place salon, this is Karen speaking, how may I help you?" "This is Denise Lincoln. Linda, please."

"She's doing a perm right now. Are you calling about the message she left you earlier, Denise?

Denise didn't have a clue what Karen was talking about; hell, she still had sleep in her voice.

"Yes, I am," Denise said, playing along and hoping not to make a fool of herself.

"So, you can come in at 12:45 today?" "Yep, sure can." "Oh, good. Linda was running a little behind. She knows how you hate waiting. I'll tell her you confirmed, okay, Denise?" "Thanks, sweetie."

Denise placed the phone back on the cradle and went to the bathroom to take a piss. The house was quiet because Sean had taken Marla with him to Toledo to visit his parents. Marla could be quite a handful at three. Knock on wood, they'd made it through the terrible twos, but it was still kind of rough. Motherhood was a necessary evil. It sounded kind of harsh, but Denise didn't give a damn. Sean was big on the family stuff. Always had been, even in high school. That's all he'd talked about: getting

41

married and having a family.

There was nothing wrong with having kids but once you had them, that was it, you couldn't give em' back. Sean and Dee had planned on two children and technically they had one more to go, though Dee had major reservations. Sean and Dee had got married right out of college before they got a chance to establish their careers. They waited awhile before conceiving Marla. Denise heard other mothers say their lives wouldn't be the same without their kids, yet Dee couldn't say that. Marla had been a blessing, yet so was life before Marla was conceived.

Sean and Dee were complete in so many ways and she enjoyed the spontaneity of that old lifestyle and missed it. They both worked in advertising. He was the local sales manager at 101. FM The Beat, an urban radio station in the New Center area of Detroit. Cyn was real cool to work for at Peachtree, and she welcomed Dee's suggestions and gave her credit when and where it was due. Plus, she was extremely generous with flextime and three weeks of paid vacation. Dee thought how far Peachtree had come and how it all came to be.

Prior to Peachtree, both women had worked in the radio industry. Cyn had been an account executive, and Dee a promotions director at a different station. Cyn got sick of busting her ass and complaining she did not go to college to be a professional hustler. After securing a small business loan and with five years of advertising experience under her belt, she finally threw in the towel and opened her own business in fall of 1995.

Initially, when Cyn started Peachtree, Dee lent a hand part time when she could. Many of Cyn's clients followed her and more arrived through word of mouth, so she started growing and had to relocate to a larger office and hire staff. The neat thing was that the girl loved to find a way to conserve money, so Cyn hired Dee, and then Cora as the office assistant, but the rest of the staff were college interns working for credits. Cyn did give them perks like comp tickets to events, movie passes and tokens like that to keep them happy. And here they were now, almost eight years later, and they'd grown to a staff of thirty-three full and part time employees. They also managed to land accounts almost daily, which was good for any business, especially a minority female-owned one.

Together they schmoozed the hell out of the clients, but Cyn had more of the Midas touch when it came to being large and in charge. Dee was convinced that this attribute stemmed from the years Cyn had spent with Bashar, but she would never say that to her. Cyn was tough as nails on the surface, though Dee knew her friend still had major scar tissue around her heart that needed to be healed when it came to Bashar Bazzi.

CHAPTER TWELVE

Commitment hadn't been an issue for Sean and Dee. Her attitude was, *either you're with me or you're not.* Dee refused to sit and wonder what Sean did when they weren't together. She'd had a few indiscretions that weren't shared with anybody other than the brother that had been lying between the sheets with her. That audience seemed to be enough. Sean was not Mr. Innocent either. Dee knew he tipped every now and then, just as she did.

Marrying young seemed a good excuse that worked for her. Dee managed to not do stupid shit, like fucking her next door neighbor. Sure, she tried hard not to screw up her stable home. Both she and Sean worked damned hard at keeping it tight. Not only that, recently, *The Michigan Chronicle*, Detroit's black newspaper, had featured them as a family on the move, something they'd worked hard to earn. People envied them because of their position. Often they were asked what their secret was. Her response was, 'Knowing when to keep your mouth shut.'

Speaking of men, Denise loved that she had herself a fine black brother. Light, dark, tall or short, it never mattered. Sean was the epitome of a strong dark-skinned GQ guy. Some of her female friends had to dress their men. Knock on wood, that chore didn't belong to Dee. Sean kept himself well- groomed, head to toe. On very little in her marriage did she have to give him direction. He held his own. She gave him his props, and he hers, but neither one of them were doormats for each other. If he was wrong about something, he got checked and he listened to her. He kept her in line too. That's what she appreciated most in her marriage.

They had been together a total of thirteen years, and at some point in their marriage, she knew that she and Sean would stop creeping out on each other. He had no clue she knew he had crept out on her earlier on in their marriage until she'd confronted his ass about it and he confessed. To this day, she never revealed to him just how she found out. Some things you didn't tell, and her unfaithfulness was one of them.

Cyn, Tavie and Vette all got down United Nations when it came to dating. The closest Dee came to it was in high school when she allowed Mitchell Fienstein to perform fellatio on her in the gym under the bleachers. The boy didn't know when to stop and he had the nerve to try and kiss her afterwards, which was totally wrong! Why in the world would she want to taste her own coochie? Dee didn't play that shit. She avoided him like the plague later, and Mitchell seemed somewhat dismayed by it. Besides, Sean would've freaked to know he wasn't the first in every sense for her, sexually speaking. The first time he ate her out was in college and he was drunk.

Dee got peeved thinking back on that because she had been going down on him since the tenth grade! And she swallowed! Personally, Dee knew her resentment came from her maternal grandmother who was White. Granny wasn't thrilled about having Black grandchildren, a fact that she never hid, God bless her soul. That's where Dee got her freckles and red hair from. And whenever she looked at herself, it was a constant reminder.

Dee's hair appointment began to creep up on her, so quickly she wolfed down two bowls of raisin bran and skim milk. Quickly showering, she pulled her wavy hair back in a ponytail, threw on some sweats and dashed off to Linda's. Pulling into the parking lot, she noticed Vette's two-toned silver and white Lexus and parked the Jag beside it. Actually, the Jag belonged to Sean but he swapped cars with her on the weekend and took the Durango.

Denise signed in, and the shampoo technician washed her hair and sat her under the dryer for twenty minutes with a protein conditioner, which helped calm down her coppery wavy mop and kept it manageable. Denise had liked to wear it in a layered blunt cut but she was starting to get bored with it, though for now it would have to do until spring. That's when she'd change it. The heat from the hair dryer made Denise drowsy and momentarily she nodded off, until she heard a knock on her dryer.

CHAPTER THIRTEEN

"Hey, sleepy head. Wake up!"

"Vette, I saw your car out back in the lot. What you getting done today?"

"Just a manicure and pedicure. Hot date tonight and these dogs of mine have to be prepped for a little love and affection. Damn, I love having my toes sucked, girl! And if I play my cards right, well, I won't go there, don't want you to be jealous," Vette joked.

"Why stop there? You're so bad. Anybody I know?"

"Ah, well, you'll just have to wait and see. Seriously though, Dee, you think Tavie and Cyn are mad at me for last night?"

"Not at all. Tavie only has Mack on the brain, and Cyn blew it off ". "Cyn totally freaked but she maintained her cool, you know our girl. Hopefully Thad took care of business last night. That Mack isn't about shit though, Denise. I swear he was real chummy with the braids chick. Tavie's gotta always watch her back with him. How fucked up is that?"

"I hear you, girl. You're right but she's not there yet, Vette. God willing, she'll take off those damned blinders and see Mack for who he is. Until then, he isn't the problem, Tavie is."

"I feel you, girl. I wish we had more time to chat, but I gotta get hooked up for tonight. I'll call you next week." With that, Vette sauntered off to the spa area of the salon, leaving Denise with a little more time under the dryer where she drifted off to sleep again.

After Dee left the salon, she headed over to her parents'

house to check in on them but they weren't home. She wrote a note to say she'd dropped by and posted it on the refrigerator. Valentine's Day was less than two weeks away and her lingerie wardrobe definitely needed a pick-me-up, so she made a beeline over to Lover's Lane. A red-hot little number with a snapped crotch caught her eye, but when she tried it on she felt it looked much better hanging on the mannequin than it did on her. Before she could began to get disappointed she spotted a similar outfit, but it had a matching thong instead of crotchless panties.

She hated thongs and didn't know what all the fuss was about. She didn't own a single pair, up until now. The sales clerk tried tempting Dee into purchasing the latest and greatest in vibrators. The tempting thing about the unique device was it had a swivel head that moved back and forth. It even came equipped with a remote control to adjust the speeds. Sean would get a kick out of watching her get off on that, though she would be faking big time! They had experimented enough for Dee to know human stimulation satisfied her more, though she took pleasure seeing Sean turned on.

CHAPTER FOURTEEN

It was after five when Dee arrived back home, and Marla was waiting to greet her.

"Mommy, Mommy, Mommy! I missed you today! You miss me?" Denise bent down, and Marla wrapped her chubby dimpled arms around her neck, hugging tightly.

"Yes, baby, Mommy missed you. Have a good day?" Dee looked at her wide-eyed daughter, who appeared to be a miniature version of her. "Yeah! Granny and Grandpa sent home an apple pie I helped make.

Can we have pizza for dinner? I'm hungry." "We can have pizza. Where's Daddy?"

"On the phone with Uncle John. He just called. Got your hair done, Mommy?"

"Yes, Marla." "I like it." "Thanks, baby."

Dee took Marla into the family room and put on a DVD for her. Remembering she'd left the Lover's Lane purchases out in the car, which she didn't want Sean to see before Valentine's Day, she sprinted out to the garage and quickly retrieved the bags from the Durango. She heard Sean laughing while talking on the phone with his older brother, John, who lived in Chicago. Sean would be tied up awhile because John was long-winded. Taking off her sweats, she freshened up and put on a Victoria's Secret emerald-color two-piece lounger. She also sprayed a sample of their fragrance, Angel Wings, which wasn't bad, but she wasn't convinced she'd buy a bottle of the stuff. Making sure her make-up was in place, she went down to the basement to say hey to her husband. Sean quickly stole a kiss from her and motioned for her to get him off the phone, but she teased him by going back upstairs. Buddy's Pizza had the best square pizza in the world, but unfortunately they didn't deliver. Marla enjoyed the ride going to pick up their order. The little girl made Denise promise her she could have a slice of apple pie for dessert. Normally, Denise didn't believe in allowing too many sweets for her child, but Marla had helped make it. Because of this, she would oblige her. It was time for to wash Marla's hair, a task performed ritually every Saturday evening. It wasn't an easy task by any means, for Marla was tender-headed and she had thick hair just like Dee's, though Marla's hair seemed to have a more golden tones versus Dee's copper ones. Sometimes Dee would get lucky. Marla would doze off early, but not tonight; her daughter was still going strong when she finished combing her hair.

Sean ate dinner with his girls and afterwards he went in to watch the Red Wings play the Black Hawks. After the game, he went into Marla's bedroom to kiss her goodnight but she wasn't there. Walking into the master bedroom, he found Marla and Denise cuddled up together asleep with the

Monsters Inc. DVD still playing. Fondly, he stared at his wife and daughter. Instantly, he became overcome with joy. He loved them, and he'd never give them a reason to think otherwise.

Sean's love had grown immensely for Dee. Not that they didn't try each other, 'cause they did. Yet they hung in there and it paid off. Next year would be their tenth wedding anniversary, for which they were planning a ceremony to renew their vows.

Sean walked over to the bed and took Marla up in his arms, carried her to her room and tucked her into bed. Dee was in a deep sleep again when he returned. Even sleeping, his wife managed to look sexy, arousing him. She was always up for some loving so he kissed her softly on her cheeks and lips until she opened her eyes and smiled. That confirmation was all Sean needed tonight. He'd give Dee something worth waking up for!

CHAPTER FIFTEEN

Vette's date turned out to be better than she thought it would be. For one, Louis Burns was an old flame. She'd met him after high school while touring as Ford's spokes model with the International Auto Show. After graduation, college had seemed to be more confining, so Vette had decided to pursue a career in modeling. She'd auditioned with Ford and they hired her to represent the Ford Tempo, back in 1989.

Most of her friends attended college right after school and went on to do great things. Vette had never had regrets about not going, because she'd had an opportunity of a lifetime that most women didn't get to do and that meant a lot to her. Cyn had auditioned with her too, and was selected, but she opted only to do Detroit's annual auto show downtown at Cobo Hall. Vette toured around with the company nine months of the year and was paid $30,000 which, thirteen years ago, was considered decent money.

Law was something that fascinated Corvette Vern, though she decided against going to law school to become a lawyer. Instead, she narrowed her choices down to a career as a paralegal or a court reporter. She'd decided on the latter. She studied her trade at the National Academy of Court Reporting and she earned her certificate in nine months. Within that time, she'd interned at Oakland County Circuit Court and honed her craft even more.

Vette owned a two-bedroom bungalow in Royal Oak, and since there was enough room in the house for her to set up an office and operate from home, that's exactly what she did. Work wasn't hard to come by. Vette networked like crazy! Additionally, she helped out the Oakland County Democratic Party, which gave her the exposure she needed to make business connections. Her workload kept her busy and permitted her to live quite comfortably.

Puffing on a Newport, Vette thought of how much her friends were a real family to her. They'd practically grown up within the same subdivision, Eaton Square in Southfield. Her mother, Tara, a surgical nurse, had already been divorced with two kids when she'd discovered she was pregnant with Vette. To top it all, Vette's father, single at the time, had gotten engaged to some woman in Boston and moved before her mother had given birth.

When her father moved away, the only thing he took with him was his '57 silver Corvette, which Vette's mother named her after. Tara claimed her labor with Vette was fast as her father's sports car; she gave birth to Vette two hours after her waters broke. Vette didn't get to really know her father as a child when she really needed him. It'd been during the last ten years that they'd bonded. Unfortunately a health crisis had brought them together. When diagnosed with prostate cancer, Vette's father suddenly got sentimental.

Vette's father married Julie, the woman he left her mom for. Later they found out Julie couldn't have children. Much of Vette's childhood went by with few phone calls from her father, unless it was her birthday or Christmas. He'd make sure he'd send something in the mail as an acknowledgment. But Vette never even got an invitation to Boston for a visit. The other thing that troubled Vette was she didn't get to meet her paternal family until a family reunion ten years ago. Her father had never told his folks about Vette because he was ashamed she was illegitimate, a fact he didn't want to taint his reputation.

ALL OF VETTE'S DISDAIN melted away when she met her father's family for the first time. They embraced her with open arms and welcomed her into the fold. As a matter of fact, she'd gotten a little too close for her mother's taste. Tara considered it a slap in the face and constantly told Vette she felt she was spitting on her grave, even though she was still alive.

Tara was not the easiest person to get along with while she

was growing up. Vette's half-siblings, Patrick and Courtney, three and five years older than her respectively, helped take care of her while their mother worked. Their dad—Tara's ex- husband—had joint custody and every other weekend he picked them up, leaving Vette behind with her mother. Tara acted as if Vette had been the one who asked to be born. She bitched a lot when she couldn't go out to party with her friends. Vette began to withdraw more and more and had to see a therapist, who recommended her mother try harder get to know her, for she was her child.

The saving grace for Vette was after-school activities and sleepovers with her classmates. Then, she got involved with cheerleading and that gave her an out during most of high school. She struck up a friendship with Tavie and Denise in junior high. Once they met,

Vette couldn't wait to start high school because she had new friends. At the beginning of freshman year at Southfield Lathrup High School, Tavie introduced them to Cyn, her neighbor from across the street, and they clicked immediately.

Vette dreaded going to Mass this morning and seeing her mother, especially after still being euphoric over last night. Louis had put a smile on her face and hopefully it wouldn't turn into a frown after spending time with her mother. Louis was one of the good guys who'd already been spoken for when Vette first met him more than a decade ago. He was twelve years her senior and today he looked well for forty-four. Vette had unexpectedly run into him in an elevator downtown at 36th District Court. However, this time around, Louis had been legally separated for two years and was in the process of filing for divorce. Louis was a fair-skinned black man with a head of salt and pepper colored hair. Vette thought it made him look distinguished and incredibly handsome.

She opted to go to afternoon Mass. Nothing compared to basking in your own glory after a night of love. Her thoughts were private and exhilarating. She relished the quiet moments of mental masturbation. Last night was the bomb! She thought back to the events and grinned. Louis had taken her to dinner at Mario's, one of the best Italian restaurants in the city of Detroit. Following dinner, they'd headed to Edison's Cigar and Martini Bar in downtown Birmingham to hear Straight Ahead, an all-ladies local jazz group.

Afterwards they'd strolled hand in hand around downtown Birmingham before they'd headed back to her place. Vette liked to say they made love, but these days, you really never knew. She felt she must be getting older because there was a time not so long ago when her only goal was for the sex to be good.

Sometimes sex could be deceiving. At times it made her strong, but then it also left her feeling empty and weak. She had been both and it bothered her tremendously. Like now, she wished she could read the thoughts in Louis's head. If she went with her gut, it would tell her to chill, but that made her uncomfortable because it'd been her experience that when you chill, you lose.

She decided to go to Whole Foods Market in Farmington Hills to pick up some organic produce. Not that she was against eating market fruit; it was just all those chemicals scared her. If she had to pay more for her groceries, she'd do it in a heartbeat.

Overall, it had been a good weekend. Vette was a sucker for romance, and so were most of her friends. Rarely did they keep secrets from one another, though now Vette found herself carrying one that she'd almost revealed Friday night. She'd tried to spill the sketchy information she had. However, seeing Cyn's reaction to just Bashar's name alone had told her it wasn't the right time for her to reveal to what little she knew. Soon, she'd have enough information to uncover the mystery. Then she'd figure out what she needed to do.

CHAPTER SIXTEEN

Mr. Sadiq phoned Vette a week after the deposition. He'd hesitated when Vette asked him about Bashar Bazzi, which made her suspicious. Vette had to admit it was one of the most awkward conversations she'd ever had in her life. You see, Vette was one of those diehard Cyn and Bashar fans. Even though she had been traveling with the auto show when they broke up, Vette assumed they would get back together eventually. The way Bashar left had baffled everybody. Vette swore, if she had been in Cyn's shoes, she might have checked in Havenwyck's Mental Hospital for an extended stay. Mr. Sadiq had the nerve to be evasive when they'd talked, which intrigued Vette more. Indifferent, Mr. Sadiq tersely said goodbye, leaving her with an uneasy feeling.

Many people told Vette she favored soap opera actress, Melody Thomas, who played Nikki Newman in *The Young and Restless*. She did have highlighted bleached blond hair. She stood 5'4 and was one- hundred and thirty-five pounds. Additionally she lucked out with a shapely pair of hips, but her bust line was another subject. Vette was self-conscious because she had these enormous nipples and small breasts. She enhanced her 34A cup by wearing water and Wonder Bras. None of her lovers ever complained and she swore to herself if they did, she'd tell them to push both of her tits together and make one big one!

Vette's face wasn't hard on the eyes either, but she felt she could use some Botox injections to remove a few lines around her eyes. She'd recently turned thirty-two but people still assumed she was in her twenties, something she never denied! Growing older didn't bother Vette. However, the reality was that the infamous biological clock was ticking loud enough to get her attention, and pretty soon she'd no longer be able to press the snooze button on her fertility.

CHAPTER SEVENTEEN

Sunday arrived and Cyn couldn't have been happier. Thad's flight was arriving this evening after being gone for two long weeks. With both of their careers in high gear, accommodation had become a major buzzword in their relationship.

Cyn spent much of the weekend preparing for Thad's homecoming, including going to Capelli's' Day Spa for some body treatments. One in particular, the dreaded Brazilian bikini wax, was a necessary evil 'cause Cyn loathed having a hairy bush. Lydia, her esthetician, had showed no sympathy yesterday while tweezing away many ingrown hairs. Cyn's pleadings fell on deaf ears as Lydia tweezed. But the temporary discomfort was well worth it, Cyn figured. Nothing could be more of a major turnoff than witnessing a man choking on stray pussy hairs.

Cyn left Capelli's feeling totally fabulous. Thank God she got her hair done yesterday. It still looked like she'd just stepped out of the salon. Cyn took pride in her hair, which extended twenty-two inches down her back. It was hard balancing her life and incorporating a solid spiritual foundation on top of everything surrounding her world, yet she made it happen. God was the only thing that had saved her from losing her mind so many years ago.

Unbeknownst to her friends and family, Cyn had walked on the edge of the darkest pit in her life and it had taken all the strength she could muster not to fall in. Sure, people pitied her, because she suffered the loss of her first love. Cyn played it off big time until she realized Bashar had permanently split. Yoga and prayer became her new loves and led her on a spiritual path that made her closer with God, which had kept her grounded up until now. As bitter as that part of her life was, Cyn acknowledged what she found in the process had made her a better woman, in spite of it.

Late afternoon following church, Cyn met her parents for dinner. Stoked about Thad's impending homecoming, Cyn thanked her parents for a delicious meal and went home to freshen up. While listening to Sade, Cyn heard her phone ring. She would be the first to admit she was a caller ID cripple. She didn't leap without looking.

"Hello."

"Hey, lady."

"Thad! Oh, honey, I missed you. Where are you?"

"I'M CONNECTING FROM Cleveland to Detroit. I'll be there soon, baby. Can't wait."

"You coming straight here?" Cyn heard Thad chuckle. "I'll see you in two hours tops, Cyn. Love you."

"I love you too. Hurry, okay?" "I will."

Thad caught his connecting flight and gazed out of the window next to his seat. Singapore had been a successful trip, yet he missed Cyn. It amazed him, the magnitude of the love he had for that woman. Take tonight; Cyn, in her beautiful glory, would be dressed to thrill and they'd be like rabbits, going at it into the wee hours of morning. Yet Thad could take her in torn jeans and a tee shirt, just as long as he had her. But that wasn't the case with Cyn. She was dramatic. Hell, Thad wouldn't be a wee bit disappointed if she hadn't prepared a private performance for two this evening. Though he knew different.

Cyn was Thad's first monogamous relationship since his split from Heather. A failed marriage had not left either party bitter; it was a matter of career choices.

Heather chose to make the Navy a career and that didn't leave room for Thad. He was not used to a nomadic military lifestyle and they chose to go their separate ways. There had been other women Thad dated noncommittally, and it had worked fine until Cyndarella Worthy came into his life. Stretching back in his seat, Thad heard the flight attendant's message on the loudspeaker announcing that soon they would be descending onto Detroit Metro airport and his heart skipped a bit. Finally, Thad sighed with relief: he was back in Detroit.

Cyn sizzled in a daring black negligee. She admired her shapely body, but she knew better than to brag. She worked out at least four times a week to maintain her physique. She lined her lips with MAC's Chestnut lip liner followed by a couple coats of O lipstick. Vanisia, a signature fragrance by the House of Creed, added the finishing touch. If any woman wanted to set the stage for seduction, this fragrance was a must-have. It had vanilla and oriental notes combined with a touch of bergamot and it drove men crazy when they smelled it on her. The stuff wasn't cheap and you had to get it from the high-end department store like Neiman Marcus or Nordstrom.

Thad arrived back in Detroit twenty minutes ahead of schedule. It gave him enough time to go home and freshen up. He was glad his business overseas had concluded successfully. Singapore had a little something, but it sucked having a language translator with you every step of the moment. Thad was multilingual. He spoke English, French and Spanish, and that was more than enough for him. He wasn't quite ready to learn anything else, nor did he feel the need to.

Making sure he hadn't forgotten the bag carrying Cyn's presents, he grabbed his keys and took off. He knew Cyn hated waiting and, speaking of waiting, he felt it was high time she handed over the key to the crib. May 21st would mark their first anniversary as a couple together and he'd given her carte blanche to any and all that he had. So had she, to a point. In case of an emergency, he did have a spare set of keys to her cars, and with Cyn that meant progress. Though, after tonight, Thad had an inkling that their relationship was going to become more definite. Distance did make the heart grow fonder. At least he hoped so.

CHAPTER EIGHTEEN

Cyn added more wood to the fire and went downstairs to lie on her ivory leather recliner. Between sips of Merlot, she popped Altoid mints like crazy. She heard Thad's Navigator pull up and promptly opened to the door before he could ring the bell. Immediately she welcomed him with a warm, long and passionate embrace.

"Baby, it's so good to hold you again. Damn, you look good, Cyn." "Now, c'mon, you weren't expecting anything less were you?" Cyn sassed.

Thad couldn't help but admire his woman. Cyn's confidence level was consistently high, a trait that he'd found few and far between in the women he'd formerly dated. They'd constantly needed reassurance, which wasn't always a bad thing. But that shit had a way of taking its toll on a brother.

"Oh my God, T-Man, you're home. I missed you."

Between kisses, Cyn took the time to hang up Thad's black leather jacket in the front closet. He walked over to the kitchen to pour himself a glass of brandy, as he secretly spied Cyn nonchalantly glancing at two bags that contained souvenirs.

"Go ahead and open them, they're for you." "Was I that obvious?" Cyn questioned. "Yeah, you're busted, lady."

"Baby, I'm terrible. I can't help it. Thank you, sweetie," Cyn cooed.

Thad handed over the goods and she took it from there. She was like a kid at Christmas as she opened each present. The first box contained a turquoise-blue dragon and tiger silk kimono. In the Asian culture, the dragon and tiger represented power that provided a level of protection from evil.

"Thad, this is so gorgeous! Oh, look at this kimono, it is *so soft!*"

"Cyn, Asian clothes tend to run smaller. Try it on for me."

She tried on the kimono for him and got his seal of approval. He sat next to her on the couch while she unwrapped the next present, a rosewood handcrafted jewelry box. When she opened one of the drawers, she found it contained a Swarovski sixteen-inch crystal and gold necklace with matching earrings.

"Oh, Thad, they're beautiful! Thank you so much. I love everything. Your itinerary was packed, so when did you find time to shop?"

"There was no way I would go Singapore and not take care of my favorite girl. You know better than that."

"You're so thoughtful, thank you for thinking of me," she offered. "Why don't you take a look in that second drawer for me?" Thad instructed a delighted Cyn.

She gasped when she noticed the stunning three-carat solitaire ring strategically placed in the jewel box. Thad officially kneeled down on one and took her trembling hand and asked her to marry him.

"Cyndarella Worthy, make me a happy man. Say you'll marry me," he proposed to his astonished lover.

"Oh my God, Thad! I had no idea this was coming. It's so soon for us? Are you sure?"

"Baby, I've never been surer of anything else in my life. We can have a long engagement if you want, but I'd like us to get married soon."

Cradling Thad's face in her hands, Cyn peered into his eyes that never left hers. Propelled by the sincerity of the proposal, jubilantly she said yes.

CYN AND THAD PLANNED an engagement party for their close family and friends on Valentine's Day. Thad opted to host the event at his West Bloomfield home where together they'd share the good news. The house was uniquely fitted out for the bash. Red and white decorations, from balloons to flowers, were found throughout. Thad wondered if people suspected what was going to go down. Not that it mattered. Most people close to him approved of Cyn. However, Cyn hadn't had an opportunity to spend much time with his mother, who now resided in Marietta, Georgia. Though they had gotten along the few times they had seen each other.

Cyn arrived prior to the guests, in a spectacular red Dolce & Gabbana corset dress, prompting Thad to request a quickie, which she declined. Marveling at the festive decorations excited her, even though she noticed Thad seemed distant after she refused his offer for a quickie. He'd get over it, she thought. Shit, it took her three hours to get dressed! That didn't include the other three hours she'd spent in the salon getting her hair styled yesterday. It took work and she was not about to mess up her make- up and hair for a screw.

Folks started to arrive as India Arie's CD played on the stereo. As the evening progressed, Cyn slipped on her engagement ring and Thad made the announcement to their delighted guests.

Willa and Vernon congratulated their daughter and future son-in-law by making an impromptu, heartfelt speech that touched the happy pair. This started a trend from the well- wishers as they toasted to an early September wedding. Cyn and Thad has chosen Labor Day weekend, mainly to give out of town guests an opportunity to stay for an extended time. Denise, Tavie and Vette checked out Cyn's rock and gave their approval. The princess-cut diamond was gorgeous. Vette took the moment to stake her place as bridesmaid, which made the other guests laugh.

"You are all my bridesmaids," Cyn affirmed. The girls wondered if Cyn had chosen a site for the reception, but she hadn't yet. Caught up in the excitement of the evening, the women didn't notice Thad approaching them. Listening to the endless chatter had started to get to him. He liked Cyn's buddies but sometimes they got on his last nerves. In particular, at the present moment, which he inadvertently let them know.

"Cyn isn't marrying herself, ladies. I too will be an active participant in the planning." Thad spoke rather patronizingly, irritating Cyn, who chose to remain silent.

Vernon Worthy nursed his sifter of cognac, while Willa mingled with the other guests. Thad's interruption did not go unnoticed by him. Nor did the look of embarrassment plastered on his daughter's face.

CHAPTER NINETEEN

School break was less than a week away and Tavie couldn't have been more jubilant. Mack had planned a mini vacation in Toronto, where they were staying at one of their favorite hotels, the Royal York. Toronto held lots of good memories for them, Tavie thought, while drinking a latte. They intended to check out a couple of musicals and some of the jazz clubs. Toronto's nightclubs mimicked New York's, but on a smaller scale. It didn't hurt that the currency in Canada was at an all-time low. For the first time in ages things had been going okay for them, knock on wood, but Tavie had learned not to get her hopes up. Raking her fingers through her hair had become a trademark of hers whenever she was antsy, which seemed constant these days.

Tavie made it a point to never take work home with her. She had almost completed checking her students' assignments and she was quite pleased with the results. Her students were excelling. The school season had gotten off to a bumpy start, because Governor Engler had decided people could send their children to any public school regardless of the county they lived in, as long as it was within a thirty-mile radius.

This did not please many parents residing in the Southfield community. Though only a certain number of students per school year were supposed to be allowed to attend each school within the district, overcrowding soon became an issue. Parents from other cities, especially the urban ones, claimed the school board had designated a racist system for allowing their children to attend the schools. Emergency meetings had to be held to calm parents in and outside the district.

Engrossed in completing her last batch of papers, Tavie didn't hear the rapping on her door.

"Hey, Octavia. How's everything going?"

"I'm fine, Mrs. Hervey. I can't wait for our break," Tavie offered.

Mrs. Hervey was Tavie's mentor. Matter of fact, she had been her fourth grade teacher. Back in the day she'd been top-notch. Some of her methods weren't always traditional, but they worked. She loved to give assignments that challenged her students on an academic level, and this was one of many reasons why Tavie had decided to become an elementary school teacher. "You planning on something special?"

"Well, actually, Mack is taking me to Toronto for a few days." Tavie spoke in an upbeat voice.

"That's nice. You could use a little rest and relaxation."
"Yeah, Mrs. H., I could."

"So, how long have you and Mack been together now?"

Shifting uneasily while seated at her desk, Tavie answered her mentor back promptly.

"Three years."

"Make sure Mack's not wasting your time," Mrs. Hervey recommended.

"We're in it for the long haul, though it's not always easy."
"Well, marriage isn't either, but couples do it everyday. It can be rewarding, even though you have to work at it."

"Honestly, sometimes I feel like I am Mrs. Mack Dooley. I do everything a wife would do and I love him, despite his issues."

"His issues will soon become your issues, Tavie. Then what?"

"I have it under control. We worked out most of the kinks, Mrs. Hervey."

Mrs. Hervey glanced inquisitively at Tavie, wondering how

someone as terrific a person as she was could be so accommodating of Mack's duplicity. It was rumored that Mack'd had a roving eye for a while. The disturbing thing was Tavie had obvious blind faith in the man.

"Okay, dear, I hear your words, but your eyes say more of what you're feeling. Women are something else when it comes to men these days. They'll do anything to snag a man, especially someone of Mack's caliber. Be careful honey. That's all."

"I will Mrs. Hervey. I'm wise to the tricks."

"Is Mack? All right, I've said my piece. Goodbye for now.

Call me at home if you need to talk."

Tavie was glad Mrs. Hervey had taken her leave. She'd turned to the older woman as her confidante, though at times her comments stung like a bee. Opening up her desk drawer, Tavie reached for the bottle of St. John's Wort capsules. Media hype about it working wonders for depression had made Tavie try it and now she was a staunch believer in the herb's medicinal benefits. To her it was like an American Express: you didn't leave home without it.

CHAPTER TWENTY

The smell of bacon permeating throughout the house that morning left Tavie reeling with queasiness. The school season had ended on a high note. All of the students had successfully completed the fourth grade. Though, of course, Tavie did have three students whose passing to the fifth grade was contingent upon the outcome of grades achieved through performance at summer school.

Tavie was usually an early bird, yet she couldn't get out of bed these days. If she did, it was to go to the bathroom where she'd be sure to toss everything in her system, which really hadn't been much lately. For the past week, stomach 'flu had decided to make her its buddy, which she didn't appreciate. Mack had gotten the bug too, and both had been miserable, but now he seemed to have beaten it. At that moment, he came in carrying breakfast in bed for her. Even though it was just breakfast, Mack presented his spread well.

"Baby, I hope your appetite's back. I made your favorites: French toast with fresh berries and whipped cream, bacon and hazelnut coffee". Tavie moved forward and placed an endearing kiss on his cheek.

"Thanks, babe. You know I love it when you're thoughtful." She spoke weakly.

Her face appeared gaunt and her eyes were puffy, Mack observed, as he looked at her with growing concern. Moreover, she must have lost at least ten pounds from her already thin frame.

"Baby, you have got to go see the doctor."

"I know. Dr. Michaels said if the prescriptions didn't work, to call for an appointment."

"Give me your plate; you can't eat if you're feeling sick. I wanted to cook breakfast for you before I left for the conference. You know they got me facilitating that workshop I've been preparing on Violence in the Public School System."

"Mackenzie, I wish I could be there, but I can't seem to shake this!" she exclaimed.

"With all that vomiting you've been doing, I doubt it if you could stand the drive. And you know your parents were looking forward to seeing you. Besides that, I don't like spending one night away from you," Mack replied.

"I know. This is the first conference I've missed in years. Oh, well!"

"Let me take the dishes to the kitchen before you make me attempt bodily harm," Mack teased. Even sick, Tavie managed to turn him on.

"Well, that's where being a gentleman comes in handy. You know what I mean. Gentle *man*," Tavie emphasized.

Mack seized the opportunity to make love to Tavie again before he drove up to Lansing. He retreated afterwards to the bathroom to shower and dress, while Tavie made her appointment to see Dr. Michaels. Luckily for her, another patient had canceled and she called just in time to get the afternoon appointment. She got out of bed and put Mack's overnight bag at the front door, along with his laptop. The Detroit Free Press newspaper sat on the porch and Tavie went to retrieve it. It was raining outside and a little cool. It was June 8th and the weather hadn't moved to the eighties yet. This was Michigan weather, take it or leave it. Escalating gas prices throughout the country graced the front headlines of the paper.

"I made an appointment with Dr. Michaels this afternoon."

"Good, you have benefits. Use 'em," Mack ordered.

"Yeah, what about your benefits, Mr. Dooley, when you plan on adding me to your policy?" Tavie said inquisitively.

"Aw, baby, you know I'm teasing you!" "I'm not."

"Look, gotta go. I'll call you tonight when I get settled. Dr.

Lake wants to go over some materials with me before the workshops begin. We'll finish our benefits chat later, baby. Love you."

Tavie was glad when the door closed and Mack was gone. She made it to the bathroom just in time to throw up again.

The rain had diminished, although it remained cool out. Tavie stayed in bed until it was time for her to get ready for her doctor's appointment. After getting into her car, she immediately rolled down the windows so the fresh air could make her feel better. Though, with the ongoing construction on Northwestern Highway, every bump in the road increased her nausea tenfold.

Upon her arrival at the doctor's office, Tavie overheard several women complain of having had the same damn flu virus she'd had now for over a week as she signed in. At least she wasn't alone.

Beth, a medical assistant, took Tavie to the exam room where she was weighed. There were two patients ahead of her, so she wouldn't have much longer to wait. While biding her time, Tavie checked her messages to see if Mack had called, but he hadn't. She closed her eyes and prayed Dr. Michaels would hurry. At that very moment, divine intervention prevailed. Dr. Michaels strolled in, and right away the physician noticed the emaciated appearance of her patient.

"Tavie. You poor dear, you're not any better. Did any of the medicine I prescribed for you help at all?"

"Dr. Michaels the Lomotil helped the diarrhea but it did nothing for the nausea. I'm dry-heaving."

"Clearly we have to find out what's going on. You've lost twelve pounds since mid-last month when you were here for your physical and that concerns me. Your last period's not charted. When was it?"

"May 27th, Dr. Michaels. You put me on Yasmin back in March.

Have you forgotten?"

"No, Tavie, I haven't. Here, lie down on the table. Was there any difference in your period last month? Heavier, or lighter, maybe?"

"Nope. It's always the same and on time, I can assure you of that."

Dr. Michaels could see her line of questioning seemed like an interrogation, but she had to find the cause of Tavie's illness.

"Is there any pain around your navel or lower right side?" "Around my right side."

"Okay. I'm going to press down in the area and see if your appendix is the culprit."

Tavie winced a bit, which was enough for Dr. Michaels to have Beth take a CBC to inspect the level of white blood cells she had in her system. Tavie might need immediate surgery if indeed it was appendicitis. Though she didn't have a fever or other symptoms of the condition, which puzzled Dr. Michaels.

The doctor had Beth collect a urine specimen from Tavie to rule out pregnancy, then Tavie sat in the exam room awaiting the results.

"Well, Tavie. There is a very valid reason why you've been ill."

"Oh damn, I've got appendicitis! How did you find out that so soon? I thought you had to send my blood to a lab."

"Your blood is being sent to a lab, but based on your urine test, congratulations are in order. You're going to be a mom."

"Whoa. A what—what did you just say?" Tavie stammered in disbelief.

"You're going to be a mom." Dr. Michaels spoke encouragingly. "There's gotta be some mistake. I never missed a pill."

"Tavie, calm down. Believe me, I'm a little surprised myself, but you are indeed pregnant."

"Please, Dr. Michaels, retest me. The results are wrong. I know it.

I'll wait," Tavie demanded.

"Tavie, your blood work is at the lab and when the results come in, then we'll have final confirmation of your pregnancy. You need to come in next Tuesday for an ultrasound so we can make sure everything is okay. But based on your last period date, you're four weeks pregnant."

"Tell me about my options," Tavie queried.

"Of course. There is adoption, or abortion. Obviously if you choose adoption—"

Tavie interrupted Dr. Michaels before she could finish. "Adoption's out. I've got my whole summer ahead of me; let me tell you what it includes. Hanging out with family and friends on Martha's Vineyard, and breaking in my new Titanium golf clubs at Myrtle Beach. Things that were planned, Dr. Michaels, which this pregnancy wasn't."

Dr. Michaels started to become irritated by Tavie's attitude. In her practice, infertility was a real issue that had started to gain momentum amongst Black women. Additionally, many of those patients would do or try just about anything to be in this woman's shoes. Yet, she still had an obligation to disclose all the details of her patient's choices.

In the state of Michigan, there was a twenty-four hour waiting period before a woman could get an abortion once she'd made a decision. Dr. Michaels further explained that Tavie would have to watch a video provided by the State about abortion and sign a release after she has reviewed it. There were two methods of abortion. A surgical abortion performed here at the office. Or she could opt for the abortion pill method. Over a two-day period, Tavie would insert two birth control pills inside her cervix and, within hours, the fetus would expel from her uterus. It's wasn't pretty and it wasn't always effective. She had to be forty-seven days or less for the procedure. It was a decision she should be making with Mack once the shock wore off.

Dr. Michaels encouraged her to involve her mate so they could make a decision on the pregnancy.

"He is going to hate me for this, I just know it! I have to talk to him and he's away until tomorrow. I can't tell him this over the phone. It's too much, besides I can't explain how I got pregnant on the pill." Reaching inside her

Coach handbag, Tavie clutched her bottle of St. John's Wort and asked if Dr. Michaels could get her a cup of water, which the older woman promptly fetched and gave to her.

"What are you taking?"

"My lifesaver, St. John's Wort. You know it helps me when I'm anxious, doc. I hate to admit it, but I never thought I could feel so low. It scares me."

"You want to tell me how long you've been taking St. John's Wort?"

"Not long. I started in April."

"We've found the reason how you got pregnant. It's your brag pill. It cuts the effectiveness of birth control pills by as much as fifty per cent. The FDA is now mandating for warning labels to be placed on each bottle manufactured and sold. This could have been prevented. That's why with each visit I ask you what vitamins or supplements you're taking because sometimes there are drug interactions, as in your case, and the results have consequences."

"I'm sorry Dr. Michaels. I believed the media hype. I didn't know it risky."

"Tavie, you're not alone, but right now, young lady, you need to go home and rest. I'll see you Tuesday morning between 10:30 and 11:00 AM for an ultrasound."

Dr. Michaels gave Tavie a prescription for prenatal vitamins and instructed her to drink lots of fluids because she was dehydrated. Giving her patient a warm hug, the physician concluded Tavie had issues other than pregnancy that she needed to tackle.

CHAPTER TWENTY-ONE

Why do bad things happen to good people? Tavie wondered to herself. After she returned home from seeing Dr. Michaels, she took a long bath and fell asleep in the tub, something she never did before.

"Damn, why are you doing this to me?" Tavie spoke to her baby while she caressed her stomach.

Mack was not going to take this well at all, and Mrs. Dooley would flip when the news got out. One of the things she loved to boast about was she had no illegitimate grandchildren. In her opinion, there were more than enough Black people degrading the race by having children without being married. The broad had even asked Tavie if she practiced safe sex; Tavie had just smiled and said, of course.

Mack's family owned three auto dealerships in Michigan and two outside of Gary, Indiana. When they were raising their children, the Dooleys had spared no expense when it came to the schools their kids attended, nor the neighborhood where they'd taken residence.

Then there were the indulgences that had included summers spent on Martha's Vineyard and ski trips in Aspen or Lake Tahoe. Mrs. Dooley controlled her children like they were her personal investments. Constantly she reminded them how fortunate they were.

Mack had received offers of more than five athletic and academic college scholarships, including Princeton and Yale, but he'd opted for Michigan State instead, which still disappointed his mother today. It didn't matter that he'd graduated at the top of his class. Tavie could only imagine what Mrs. Dooley would say about the pregnancy. Mrs.

D. would swear it was planned to trap her little boy because he hadn't married Tavie yet. The thing that confounded Tavie was she wasn't exactly what you'd consider trailer trash. Her parents had raised her in a respectable suburban neighborhood, and they had a cabin up north at Idlewild where a lot black families hung out during the summer. The Slades were a working class, blue-collar family but Tavie wasn't ashamed. Her mother had worked on the assembly line at Ford and her father had been a foreman and UAW union leader for Chrysler before he retired. The first time Mack had introduced Tavie to Mrs. Dooley, Tavie would never forget the comment the other woman had made.

"A home girl with an education! What did you say her name was, son? Girlfriend? Oh, I remember now: Octavia. Forgive me!" she'd quipped.

Mack and his younger sister, Jade, laughed. Jade had even joked that her mother had the best sense of humor.

"Mrs. D. can kiss my pregnant ass!" Tavie uttered aloud to herself, while enjoying a cup of hot chocolate. She swore she'd never fuck with St. John's Wort again.

That evening, rain showers included rumbles of thunder that made her jumpy. She hated being alone during a storm. It was almost a quarter after seven, if she left now, she could be in Lansing before nine and she could tell Mack the news. As Fate would have it, at that very moment, the telephone started to ring.

"Hello."

"Hey, baby girl, feeling better?" Mack asked.

"Yes and no. Listen, I was just about to call you. I'm driving up.

What room are you in?"

"Tav, you're not driving up here in this weather while you're sick. It's storming outside and you hate driving in the rain. The conference is over tomorrow. I'll be home in the evening."

"Yeah, about my condition. Mack I need you to talk to. You don't understand. I'm scared," Tavie whispered into the mouthpiece.

"Baby, I know you're scared of storms but you'll get through it. My signal is getting weak. I'll see tomorrow, okay?"

"Hell, no, it's not okay. Mack, you're not taking me seriously. Please don't treat me like a child."

There was silence at the other end of the phone, as Mack's signal had died. For a moment, he felt compelled to leave and calm Tavie but, hell, he had one more commitment to fulfill before the school year ended completely for him. Tavie would just have to wait, he decided, sipping on a scotch and soda. It was only one night anyway, for crying out loud. Besides, the savoring hungry glances tossed his way from women passing by had distracted him. They required his immediate attention. For a moment guilt struck him, but it was short-lived, thanks to a familiar acquaintance who seductively sashayed by him. Mack waited for a while before he stalked his prey, to make her sweat a little. By now, he recognized her signals and he was buying.

CHAPTER TWENTY-TWO

It was almost 8:30 P.M., still light outside, as Tavie sped down the I-96 highway. Mack wouldn't be pleased that she'd driven up in the rain, but once she'd explained everything, he'd understand. Smiling, Tavie thought it was sweet of him to be concerned about her being afraid during the storm and wanting to protect her. Goodness, the man could be considerate. "Let me remember that to add to the reasons on my Why I love Mack list," Tavie thought aloud to herself. The list had started to get longer over the past two months and she couldn't have been happier. Finally, she could let her guard down, for Mack had changed his ways. Or at least he had seemed to have mended them.

This pregnancy was not a welcome addition to their lifestyle. "If only it would have happened next year!" she groaned, for she was sure Mack was going to propose to her soon. At least, by then they would be engaged or maybe even married. She didn't want to parade around her students as a pregnant, unmarried woman. That was not a message she wanted to send to them, despite the fact most of the kids she taught came from single parent families. She wanted better for herself, and them.

Being caught up in a traffic jam of her compulsive thoughts caused her to nearly miss her exit. The Hyatt was a lovely hotel, but the valet parking line was way too long. Pissed off, she pulled into a space towards the end of the lot, which meant she would have to walk and she had the nerve to be wearing high heels. Making her way to the front desk with her overnight bag in tow, she realized the clerk was going to give her a hard time until she flashed her credentials and driver's license which bore the same address as her man. She looked at the girl behind the counter and wanted to scream, but she stayed cool.

"We take precautions with every guest, Ms. Slade. Enjoy your stay," the front desk clerk said politely.

Key in hand, Tavie waited for the elevator and noticed the number of people mingling in the lobby. She hoped not to be recognized tonight. The elevator opened and she pressed the button for the thirteenth floor and watched each number light up as she ascended. Of course now the nausea had began to pick up speed, rearing its ugly head. Thank goodness she would be in the room soon! The elevator opened and Tavie stepped out, looking at the arrows pointing in the direction of various room numbers. She slowed her pace when she noticed a couple affectionately carrying on as they strolled down the hall ahead of her. Any passerby could see the two were in serious lust and were anxious to get to their room. Tavie wasn't mad at the sister because the brother man had good taste. His sharp beige linen suit could've been a duplicate for a similar suit Mack owned. The very thought stopped her dead in her tracks.

"Oh fuck!" Tavie muttered to herself.

The woman's shoulder-length, tied, zillion braids were pulled back in a ponytail. Tavie's heart started racing and she shook her head. No, surely that wasn't Mack? She turned down the aisle towards the room, where she got the shock of her life. The man in question was indeed Mack and he was exchanging serious tongue action with that skanky bitch. The sight sent Tavie reeling. If that wasn't enough, she recognized the woman's laughter as that of a Caribbean teacher she knew. Geneva! She used to substitute at the same school Tavie worked at and they never got along.

Geneva had taunted her about her relationship with Mack and shamelessly flirted with him whenever they attended in district school meetings. Tavie couldn't believe Mack was publicly groping Geneva's body out in the open so that most everybody at the convention would get to know they were an item! As Tavie peered around to steal a peek, the pair managed to enter his room, closing the door behind them and leaving Tavie distraught.

Denial came back to bite Tavie in her ass at a time when she didn't need it. Sure, she'd confronted Mack about cheating, and he'd lied again and again. The repetitious pattern had spiraled out of control, though she'd never listened to her gut, which had said he'd never change. Instead she'd got caught, lost between the sheets where the bed served center stage for Mack, because, hell, he gave a grand performance and she played the part of such an attentive fan. Vette had warned her to watch her back. Now, she was carrying his child. Instinctively, Tavie's hand found her stomach.

She rushed to the huge ficus plant in the corner of the hall and lost the remains in her stomach. Everything weighed on her shoulders right now and her breathing began to get erratic. Being asthmatic, she remembered her inhaler was out in her vehicle's glove compartment. Frantically she pressed the elevator's down button and hoped she hadn't been spotted soiling the plant pot. For sure, if the Hyatt had security cameras, she'd be found out.

After grabbing some water from a fountain, Tavie dashed back to her car, retrieving her inhaler before an attack came on. Between puffs, bitter tears flowed continuously. Irrespective of the hurt she felt, Tavie wasn't surprised, more disappointed. Every one around her knew what was up. Vette was right. The thing that made it even worse was now she was pregnant and in her heart she wished the baby would go away on its own, but she knew without question what had to be done. In the few seconds she saw Mack and Geneva, the reality hit her that this was what life with him would be like. All lies! She pressed the speed button on her phone and dialed Cyn's number. She hoped her friend would be there to answer.

CHAPTER TWENTY-THREE

Cyn tended to a fragile Tavie after the loss of her baby. Tavie had arrived five nights ago, frantic as all hell as she recounted to Cyn how her day had literally gone from sugar to shit within a matter of hours. Cyn tried to calm her hysterical friend, because it wasn't good for her or the child she was carrying. While screaming at the top of her lungs that she didn't want Mack's bastard inside her, Tavie doubled over in pain, and Cyn had to rush her to St. Joseph's Hospital where she suffered a miscarriage. Tavie was kept in overnight for observation because she was dehydrated as a result of hyperemesis gravid arum, caused by the pregnancy. More than anything, Tavie begged Cyn to not share the news with Denise or Vette just yet. She wanted to keep it between just the two of them. Cyn couldn't agree. She knew Tavie's spirits were low and she'd refuse to see anyone. But, ready or not, Tavie had to face the music with her friends. Regardless of Tavie's objections Cyn invited Dee and Vette over, and hoped in time that Tavie would forgive her.

Cyn's condo was carefully decked out in ivory throughout. Rarely did she allow entertaining in her home because of its designer décor. Tavie didn't blame her. She couldn't imagine having off-white carpeting. It picked up every damn thing and she wouldn't make the time to care for it like Cyn. Shit, Cyn kept a housekeeping service on call because she was too damn lazy to clean herself!

It had been days since Tavie had felt like herself. The miscarriage was a blessing in disguise, but it still hurt. She instantly felt a pang of emptiness. The music of smooth jazz softly played and she heard laughter downstairs. She borrowed one of Cyn's Victoria's Secret jersey-knit loungers and ran a comb through her hair a few times before heading downstairs.

"Hey, y'all. It ain't go no party up in here without me!" Tavie spoke. Startled by Tavie's appearance, Dee and Vette both glanced at Cyn, who looked away nonchalantly with a blank expression on her face. "Hey, yourself. Why are you wearing Cyn's pajamas?" Denise questioned.

Tavie sat down on the floor in the living room and her friends followed suit. Tavie told them all about Mack and the women were stunned. They could barely contain their loathing for the man.

"That lying dirty motherfucker! It's a shame you had to find out that way, Tavie. I'm so sorry. He had the nerve to call my house looking for you!" Vette spat.

"He called me too! I asked him if everything was okay, because he sounded like he was so goddamned worried. And all this time he was fucking around on you like that! Girl, I'm so sorry!" Denise said, as she embraced her friend.

"Me, too!" Vette added.

"Are you really sorry, Vette? I mean, don't you really want to say, I told you so? I'd deserve it. You warned me. I should've listened to you."

"Tav, it's not like that. You've suffered enough."

"Girl, please tell me you're not going back to him?" Dee pleaded. "No, I'm not. I can't. I'm drained."

"Tavie, you got to face him again. You live together. You can't stay with Cyn forever," Vette commented.

"I got a plan. I left a message for him at home that I would see him tomorrow at the golf tournament we were supposed to play in. Trust me, he will be there. That'll give me a few hours to grab my things while he's gone. I instructed the moving company to be prompt."

"Why is it men are never satisfied? I don't get it. You've been with Mack a long time. You're smart, educated and beautiful. I don't get it!" Vette wondered.

"I guess we will never know. I mean, look at Halle Berry and Eric Benet. She's a doll, but he went out and stuck it to someone else. She went on Oprah saying he'd even messed around with one of her friends. Talk about betrayal!" Dee spat words of venom.

"And to think his dick was *the* only dick you've been fucking. It's a waste. Tavie, I'm sorry, I know how that sounds, but why give a jewel to someone who doesn't give know the value?" Cyn interrogated.

"Who you telling! I love Sean dearly, but my momma didn't raise a fool here either," Dee exclaimed.

"Dee, you ain't saying Sean's cheated on you?" Tavie demanded. "Who said it had to be *Sean* doing the cheating? I'm not going to ever be one of those women who swears what their man won't do, because most times, much as I hate admitting it, they're doing it." The women were somewhat baffled as Dee continued, "They don't look at it as infidelity or cheating until you bust them. They view getting pussy as another notch on their belt."

Tavie suddenly found herself disagreeing with Denise. In her opinion, every man was not a dog. "Denise, all men don't cheat. The majority, yes, but not all. I mean look at Thad; I don't think he's cheated on Cyn, nor does he want to. It's about Cyn Worthy and they're secure." "Tavie, that's my point. Don't fall into the security trap. You'll set yourself up for more heartbreak. Thad recognizes he has a good woman in Cyn, but I doubt if Cyn's insecure," Dee advised.

"You got that right. A man's actions are his words. Forget everything else they say verbally. Things never go the way you plan them. I'm getting married much later than I thought and to someone other than Bashar."

"So, Cyn, other than race, what's the biggest difference would you say between Bashar and Thad?" a suddenly curious Vette asked.

"I'd have to say, their tempers. Bashar would never go to bed angry. He refused. Sometimes we'd stay up late into the night talking things through. Thad will argue and hold a grudge, even after we've made up."

"So could you go to bed mad at Thad when you get married?"

"I haven't lived with another man since Bashar, so I can't answer that. We'll work through it like most married people, I guess."

Vette looked at her friend beaming when she spoke of Bashar. God, was it possible that Cyn still loved Bashar? Vette couldn't help thinking.

CHAPTER TWENTY-FOUR

Laughter filled the air as the evening progressed. Cyn was speechless listening to her friends as their mirth grew louder. Between the laughs, Cyn's catered takeout dinner didn't go uneaten, nor did her well stocked bar go undrunk, as the women continued to commiserate with Tavie's plight.

"If I didn't have a good one, I'd say men ain't shit!" Dee spat.

"Sean would kick your ass if he heard you say that. You can't even go there," Cyn chided her friend.

A slightly drunk Tavie seemed open to discussing her pain. "I knew about the other women Mack had. I stayed because of the *potential* we had as a couple, you know? The *potential!* Y'all feel me? We had so much in common, and I loved him. I don't know why, I just did," she moaned.

"Girl, ain't nobody blaming you for being in love. You tried like hell to make the shit work with that Negro and look where it got you," Dee argued.

"For all it's worth, you're not the first woman whose been fucked over. We've been there and trust me, I'm not going back, thank you very much!" Cyn said, holding her hand up and displaying her engagement ring as a reminder.

"Oh, shucks, that's right, there's a bride-to-be in the house tonight. Hey, this is the last time we'll have our get-together with you as a single lady," Vette exclaimed.

Tavie found the timing was perfect to offer up a toast. "Let's honor Cyn, for tonight and for always. Love you, girl." The women clinked their glasses in agreement.

"I still can't believe I made it this close to the altar," Cyn gushed.

"You *have* been close to the altar, but we all know how it ended," Tavie suggested.

Cyn sucked in her breath, noticeably peeved.

She cleared her throat, and the spotlight returned to the miffed woman. She insisted they did not dare go back down memory lane. "Those memories won't follow me. I didn't leave a forwarding address," announced the bride-to-be.

"Cyn, I still can't believe Bashar dissed you like that. He didn't even say goodbye. Must be some Chaldean thing. You know, I hear they can be ruthless," Dee suggested.

"Cyn, do you ever wonder what happened to Bashar? I'm with Dee that it doesn't make sense," Vette prodded.

Cyn replied that, like them, she was in the dark. She had no clue. "Hey, the Desert Storm song, y'all remember? I loved this song, it was the bomb!" Tavie mouthed. Oleta Adam's old- school jam, *Get Here*, played in the background.

"Speaking of Desert Storm, Cyn, wasn't that around the time Bashar went over to the Middle East?" Vette started up again.

"It was too long ago for me to remember. And damn it, let's keep it that way! I try not to think about what might have been. That works best for me."

"Yeah, I hear you, girl," Vette nervously chimed in, hoping it went unnoticed how uncomfortable she'd become.

CHAPTER TWENTY-FIVE

Mack had considered calling the cops when Tavie went missing. She'd always returned his phone calls before. Today, though she'd said she'd meet him at the golf tournament, so he knew she was coming home, and he was going give her a piece of his mind for worrying him. Then, she was a complete no-show at the course. He hated being stressed over anything, especially Tavie. There were several of the woman's personal belongings missing from the house, yet all the furniture remained in place. He glanced at the wall clock and thought back to his last conversation with her, which gnawed at him. She said she was scared, but why? Mack had assumed it was because of the thunderstorm, but what if he was wrong? What if his woman had some life-threatening illness? He felt remorse for his actions with Geneva, who wasn't worth his sacrificing his relationship with Tavie for. They ultimately had gotten it right. He was ready to take things to the next level. Envisioning Tavie saying yes to his proposal of marriage delighted him, which took the load off the guilt of his one- night stand.

Throughout his years of dating, Mack had numerous women propose marriage to him after the first date. Yet, his Tavie only recently started tossing hints his way. Shit, like adding her to his benefits, which made Mack chuckle as he continued to wait on her arrival. Within moments, he heard the familiar sound of the automatic garage door opening up. Jumping to his feet, Mack prepared to greet her, but there was a distinct chilliness in her behavior as she walked into the room. She seemed to be caught off-guard by seeing him, and he was caught off-guard by her conduct too.

Placing her keys and garage door opener on the cocktail table, Tavie turned around to face the man whom she'd thought she'd spend the rest of her life with. Then she felt his hand on her shoulder. Animosity brewed inside her as she yanked away from his touch.

Confused, Mack demanded an explanation from her. He got more than he bargained for. Motionless, he listened as she recounted the events that had led to her disappearance and he was desolate. Sadness saturated Tavie's voice, yet she didn't shed a tear, which was just the opposite of him. He wiped his eyes, but he couldn't wipe away the guilt that ate away at him, nor did he try. Tavie made her intention to leave him clear. She wanted nothing more to do with him or hear anything he had to say, which was little. How could he? There weren't enough words in the vocabulary to save him now. They agreed on a time for her to come back and get the rest of her belongings. Before she left, he pulled her close to him and told her how sorry he was and how much he loved her. In time he hoped she would forgive him. Yet could he ever forgive himself ?

CHAPTER TWENTY-SIX

Saturday arrived faster than Vette thought it would. She'd set time aside to hang tight with Cyn, as a way of bonding with her before the wedding stuff kicked into high gear. The hard part of it meant not including Denise and Tavie, because they did every damn thing together. So, indeed, this would be quite special. Vette hated being selfish and failing to extend an invite, she thought, while chewing her bottom lip. Essentially speaking, Vette knew Cyndarella was the glue that cemented their friendship. She was the center of their universe. Not that she needed to be, but she appointed herself by deed, time and time again. It never mattered what crisis arose, or how, the girl remained a true rock.

Vette couldn't recall a time when Cyn had passed judgment on anybody. She listened intently, and then told you how it was and she moved on. Denise fell right in line with that program, too, but Tavie was the weakest link of the bunch. Vette grunted, finding it hard to sympathize with the ole girl about the Mack predicament. The bad thing for her was Tavie knew about it. Vette had warned her about the braids chick, but Tavie had taken Mack's word for it as usual. Oh, and camping out at Cyn's bit was tacky, even though Tavie had stayed—if memory served Vette correctly—less than two weeks.

Cyn needed to stay upbeat, focusing on her wedding preparations. Instead, she'd hung out with Tavie's dumb ass. Vette would have done the same thing, and wished Tavie would have come to her or Denise. Cyn had enough going on with the wedding. Vette loved Tavie, but sometimes she got on her last nerves playing the fucking victim role. Maybe it had something to do with her being an only child and having her way on a whim. Vette really didn't know why, but reasoned Tavie required psychotherapy in a big way.

Vette had earned the nicknames of Gossip Queen and Big Mouth, and, for the most part, they rang true. she looked on gossip as free entertainment. No tickets needed for admission, just enter at your own risk. It was just part of her personality. Yeah, Vette contemplated, she'd intentionally used bits of information to her advantage, but she never tried to hurt anyone.

Gossip was only good when something positive was extracted from it. She shied away from drama.

Confrontations were not her style. Vette had been through some shit, like most people, at the hands of some ruthless motherfuckers. When she gossiped, you would think she was referring to common folk unrelated to her, but that wasn't the case. Her family had sold her out in a number of ways. She chose not to revisit those painful times. Besides, it was long ago. Blood or no blood though, she'd make sure lightning didn't strike twice. Life was about personal growth, which made her ecstatic about becoming a mother. She had much to share and didn't see why she hadn't thought of doing this foster parent thing earlier.

Like every other woman, Vette assumed that by the time she hit thirty she'd have a husband, or at the least be engaged. Yet it hadn't happened that way for her. She'd had been involved in a few long-term relationships but they'd fizzled once the M word came into play. Her former lovers had started to backpedal. One ex-boyfriend had even told her that he wanted to be with her forever and have children, but if she needed a piece of paper to prove his love, it wasn't happening. One of the talents men lacked was mindreading. Vette didn't get it until much later, that she compromised herself by not stating what her needs were at the beginning of a relationship.

The truth shall set you free or hold you in bondage. The weight of those words made Vette's stomach twinge with apprehension.

She secured a reservation at one of the finest day spas in the country, the Green Door at the Somerset Collection. From the moment they entered the eucalyptus-scented spa, Cyn and Vette were given the royal treatment. Even though their appointments were scheduled together, they were taken to private adjoining rooms to get massages. Vette heard Cyn squeal with delight, "Ooh, this feels so good!"

The paraffin wax manicure and pedicure hit the spot for both of them, making their hands and feet baby-soft and smooth. Vette made it out the door without purchasing those fancy high-priced creams and things the spa estheticians recommended for one's skin type. She wouldn't have minded buying that marine-based shea butter moisturizing lotion, but at $43, it wasn't in her budget. Not to mention the matching eye cream. This afternoon, she'd had a good time. Would she be able to say the same after dinner?

Speaking of which, where in the hell was Cyn anyway?

Vette pondered in a corner booth at J.

Alexander's. They were supposed to meet at 5:15 and it was almost that now. If she didn't hurry up, Vette considered ordering one of each thing on the menu and putting it in on Cyn's tab. Before Vette could finish her thought, Cyn hurried over to the table carrying a gift bag from the spa.

"Sorry, I'm late. You been waiting long?"

"Nah, a few minutes, but tell that to my stomach. I'm starved. I see they got you, huh? What did you get?"

"Actually, Corvette, this is for you." Cyn handed Vette the gold gift bag across the table.

"Damn girl, you shouldn't have!" Vette said.

"But I did, Vette. Go on, open it," prodded Cyndarella. Vette reached inside, and there was the Sothys marine-

based moisturizing lotion and age-defying eye cream that she had considered purchasing earlier.

"Cyn, thank you so much lady! There is no way I could have afforded it right now."

"You are quite welcome, my friend. I wanted you to have a memento of the day. Vette, it was definitely right on time and I appreciate it," Cyn chirped.

"YOU KNOW, CYN, IT'S hard to believe, but in a seven weeks, you'll be Mrs. Thaddeus Mitchell! How does it feel?" Vette inquisitively asked with excitement.

"Weird as hell. You know I had practically given up on marriage. Man, you know better than anyone does. Girl, I didn't believe the right one would ever find me, but thank God, he sent Thad."

The ribs arrived and both Cyn and Vette cleaned their plates. Vette knew the evening was winding down and she could no longer stall for time without making Cyn suspicious.

"You know Cyn, I'm horrible at keeping secrets."

"No shit. That ain't nothing I don't know. So who or what is it this time?" Cyn quipped sarcastically.

"You're the one holding the lucky winning ticket." Vette began strumming her fingers on the table nervously.

"Why do you seem to believe I am in luck? And you're nervous. Stop strumming your fingers! Come on, what's it about this time? I'll come across and slap you if you got dirt on Thad."

"No, Thad has nothing to do with this. It's—"

Before she could finish, Cyn jumped in. "Let me guess, Vette, don't tell me you're on about Bashar again. I told you to leave it alone!"

"Cyn, don't get upset. I did leave it alone but then I found out something. Look, I can keep it to myself if you want me to, but whether you like it or not, you need to hear this. It'll give you closure. It's on you."

"If it's on me, it's because you couldn't mind your own damned business. You see how happy I am, and now you go behind my back and do this. Go on, out with it."

Cyn sulked, glaring at Vette, who was afraid to look at Cyn because if looks could kill, Vette would be six feet under.

Vette had hired a private investigator to find out what really had gone down. Just as she thought, it was huge. Immigration officials at the Saddam Hussein airport in Baghdad took Bashar into custody for weeks because he was Arab-American, and then it got even more twisted. Because Bashar was born outside America, there was nothing the United States could do to make the Iraqi officials release him. They locked him in one of those gruesome prisons, holding him four years before they negotiated a settlement with his family for his release.

Cyn could not believe what she was hearing. Somehow, she couldn't register Bashar being imprisoned. Nothing was criminal about him. All kinds of thoughts sped through her mind.

"How long have you known this?" Cyn demanded from a cautious Vette, who went on to explain that she'd known for about a month. She had found out by accident. It started with the Sadiq deposition. She'd told Cyn about that. What disturbed Vette even more was the follow up conversation she had with Mr. Sadiq. Vette told Cyn the investigation file was now hers to keep. She would retrieve it out of her car when they got ready to leave. All the same, Vette had to warn her. "Prepare yourself, Cyn. There were pictures taken by American Embassy officials when Bashar was released and they were graphic. Bashar got hurt. "

CHAPTER TWENTY-SEVEN

The news hit Cyn like a ton of bricks. It felt like an elephant was sitting on her chest. She had convinced herself Bashar had betrayed her. It became part of her motivation for going on to show him she'd survive despite him. Vette continued on with her story.

"You'll probably read about this in the report. When Bashar was released, the only items he wanted back of his personal belongings were two things: a picture of his mother and the other of you."

Leaving the restaurant, Cyn barely remembered Vette giving her the dossier. Driving down the highway, everything seemed foggy. Cyn arrived home and rested the back of her head against the front door when she got inside the house, hoping the spinning in her brain would stop. Almost an hour had passed, yet she couldn't muster enough nerve to read the file Vette had given her, which now lay on her desk. Every so often, she'd glance in its direction, hoping it would, by some metaphysical force, either fall into her manicured hands effortlessly, or just disappear into thin air. Not being one for wimping out on anything, she finally gained her bearings and started reading the detailed report and was floored. Vette had been right on the money.

There were official government files and clippings about Bashar's capture and imprisonment. The contents were so graphic, detailing the horrific prison environment Bashar had been subjected to for years. Cyn continued to read despite her tears which, at times, seemed to blind her. There was no way she had the strength to read the whole thing, especially seeing Bashar's snapshots that the officials from the American Embassy had taken of him, wounded and bruised.

She'd become so distressed that she had run into the bathroom, where she vomited uncontrollably. She flushed the toilet, then went to the sink and washed her face and hands. After drying them, she went into the bedroom to retrieve some medicine when her phone started ringing.

Sounding somewhat flustered Cyn answered the phone. "Hello?" "Baby, it's almost ten o'clock. Why aren't you here? You and Vette got wasted, didn't you?" Thad asked, amused.

"Oh, Thad, I'm sorry. I came back home just to freshen up a bit when, all of a sudden, one of my famous migraines kicked in. Not to mention I just finished puking my guts out.

Can we see *Crash* another day? I could really use some rest."

"Cyn, I'm coming over right now to take care of my baby girl. I figured something was wrong when you didn't answer your cell phone." "Thad, you don't have to come over tonight. I really wish you wouldn't. I promise you, I'm going straight to bed after I hang up on you. Thanks for the offer."

"Listen, I'm staying with you tonight, that's final, but I got to leave early for my golf tournament in the morning. See you in a bit."

"Alright. I tried to warn you this isn't the best time for you to come over, but you insist. I'll see you in a few. Love you.

"I do insist! I'm not trying to get laid. I just want to be with you. Relax."

Cyn felt like a trapped animal. Here she was, a grown woman, in her own house and her man would not take no for an answer. There were times when you needed to be alone and this was one of them. Maybe if she'd told him she had diarrhea and was shitting all over the place, then he would have kept his ass home, she huffed. She took two tablespoons of Pepto-Bismol and a Maxalt melt for her migraine. She locked Bashar's file in the file cabinet and headed upstairs.

Thad remembered Cyn's migraines made her sensitive to light. That explained the darkness inside her home. When he climbed to the top of the staircase and strolled into her bedroom, she was already asleep and he chose not to wake her. He smiled when he checked the alarm clock and noticed she had set it for a 5:15 A.M. for him. He quietly disrobed, got into bed, and with the remote control, turned on the television to watch the local news and *Nightline*, before he himself drifted off to sleep.

CHAPTER TWENTY-EIGHT

Cyn awoke conflicted. It was a miracle she'd gotten any sleep after learning about Bashar. She spotted a note from Thad that she read. Skipping breakfast, she recovered Bashar's file, then picked up off where she'd left off last night. Thoughts of Bashar had been stored away inside a compartment that she'd never wanted reopened. Bashar Bazzi had been her first and only love for a long time. He'd loved her and devastated her like no other man in her life ever had. It had taken years for her to actually come to the realization that their relationship was not meant to be. He had been her first, and naively she thought, her last. This news was unsettling to her. This information couldn't be swept under the carpet.

In retrospect, digging herself out of self-pity hadn't been an easy task, yet she'd managed day by day to get it right personally and professionally. She'd used her beauty to manipulate men and she loved the power it gave her. There were a few meaningful relationships along the way, but Cyn had been robbed of her innocence, leaving her unable to trust anyone. She despised Bashar for making her so bitter. Though he'd been out of her life for what seemed like forever, it was hard for her not to become angry when she thought of him, until now. Looking at Bashar's pictures troubled her. He appeared so lifeless and frail. And his eyes, those beautiful green eyes she'd adored, had no life in them either. "Oh, God," she thought to herself; Bashar's eyes then reflected what she now felt inside.

She collected herself after showering, but realized she needed further answers. Bashar had been released in 1995. Why hadn't he contacted her? And his family, Cyn thought with disgust; why didn't they have the decency to tell her what happened to their son, knowing what he'd meant to her? Cyn recalled the number of times she went to his parent's home and was ignored. They changed their phone number to avoid her calls.

Too many people had played games with her life and it was going to stop. For a moment she thought of calling Vette's private investigator to locate Bashar, but suddenly an idea popped into her head. She knew just the person who would lead her to the man in question.

CHAPTER TWENTY-NINE

Cyn walked into Fascinating Fashions in the Crosswinds Mall in West Bloomfield. The clothes were sharp but expensive, which didn't matter because the only things she was shopping for were answers, and she wasn't leaving without them.

"Oh my God, Cyndarella, you come! How are you?" Wiyad exclaimed, when she spotted her cousin's former lover.

"I know about Bashar," Cyn announced.

Wiyad studied Cyn, and she knew the woman standing before her was in an agony of the worst kind—betrayal. Wiyad removed Cyn's tortoiseshell Gucci sunglasses and revealed the woman's reddened, swollen brown eyes. Momentarily excusing herself, Wiyad spoke to her small staff, informing them she would be in a meeting with a friend and didn't want to be disturbed. With a beckoning hand, she took Cyn into her office.

"I'm sorry, Cyn. Tell me, when you find out?" Wiyad asked in broken English.

"It doesn't matter, Wiyad. I saw you months ago, why didn't *you* tell me?" Cyn asked.

"Dear Cyn, my heart broke for both you and Bashar, you know? In our culture, we take care of our own."

"Wiyad, you were like a sister to me, closer than anyone in your family ever was to me. I need answers. I'm not leaving here without them." Cyndarella's defiance alarmed and unsettled Wiyad as she resumed, "I don't want to disturb Bashar's life, believe me. I didn't come here for that, but he owes me an explanation. You must understand that."

"Of course I do. You are being fair and I will help, but, Cyn, trust me, I have to do it my way. Give me a number where I can contact you. It may take some time getting hold of Bashar, you know."

"Why, is that? Is he here in the U.S.?"

"He's here, just not Michigan. He's never come back home to our ever-loving Great Lakes State. It was too hard for him."

"Like he was the only one hurt. Wiyad, excuse me, but what about the pain inflicted on me? Or is that something you neglected to remember?"

"Oh, Cyn, you will make yourself angrier with that kind of talk. And what will it accomplish for you? Nothing at all! I will help you somehow. Give me time to arrange something."

Cyn glanced at a sample lavender dress hanging on the mannequin in the corner of Wiyad's crowded small office, which was gorgeous, with elaborate detailing. Nonetheless, whimsically, she looked away.

"I designed it myself and you'd look beautiful in it. Tell me your size," Wiyad gently prodded.

"Six."

"I'll design for you as a wedding present. Now, go get some rest," Wiyad gently pleaded. "My friend, you look like you lost your best friend." Immediately, she regretted her words. "Cyndarella, I shouldn't have said that. Forgive me."

"It's okay. You didn't say anything wrong because I did lose my best friend."

Wiyad embraced Cyn and again reassured her she would phone soon. Cyn left, and Wiyad dialed Bashar at home, but got his voicemail where she left a message, though she didn't stop there. Calling his cell phone,

Bashar answered only to be stunned with the news that he'd dreaded hearing. The time had finally come for him to face the past. He couldn't escape it. He went home, packed a suitcase and got in his car. He didn't know which flight he was headed out on to Detroit, but he'd make sure he would be on the first available.

CHAPTER THIRTY

Denise noticed Cyn was distracted. They discussed business issues. However, the rest of their conversation was small talk. Denise went into Cyn's office and closed the door. Cyn stared out the window, not really recognizing Denise was even there.

"Cyndarella Worthy, what's going on here? You're not yourself today."

Crushed, Cyn burst out in tears. After swearing Denise to secrecy, she explained her situation. She relayed the past few days to her friend, and Denise was fit to be tied.

"I could kill that bitch for telling you this shit. That peroxide has gone to her brain! Look at you, you're a wreck, Cyn, leave this alone. You know all there is to know. Put your energy into your wedding, or have you forgotten it's literally right around the corner?"

"Yeah, I have forgotten for the moment, Dee. The show will still go on, but I've got to take care of this first. I've got to."

"Does Thad know?" "No."

"Cyn, has this changed your feelings about marrying him?" Denise asked cautiously.

"I'm anything but crazy! But I do feel weird in some way. I can't begin to explain it."

"Okay, you need me to break it down for you as only a friend can do," Denise said carefully. "Your first love was the real deal, girl. Bashar truly loved you, and every bad thing you said about him for leaving has been erased by the truth, which hurts. But you're a big girl, an *engaged* one on top of that." Dee advised her to please keep that in mind. "Hey, speaking of which, the bridesmaids' dresses are in. I go for my fitting this evening. Come with me?"

"No, Denise, I can't. I'm working late tonight. Sorry for dumping my problems on you."

"Cyn, I'll kick your ass for saying some dumb junk like that. I'm always here for you. I know how you must feel, but suck it up. You've got a lifetime of happiness headed your way. I need to get back to work." The two women hugged and Denise left.

Denise called the bridal salon to see when the other bridesmaids were going in for their fitting. Dee knew Tavie had gone down to Hilton Head for a golf tournament; Vette on the other hand was another story. She'd be in tonight, which couldn't have pleased Dee more. Cyn was on the verge of losing her mind and who could blame her? Dee was going to give Vette an earful for pulling this. What was she trying to prove? Bashar didn't deserve what happened to him, but he'd made it out alive and had never felt the need to reach out to Cyn. Hopefully he wouldn't change his thought-pattern now.

Vina St. Fran

CHAPTER THIRTY-ONE

Denise loved how regal she looked in her Vera Wang gown. She winked in appreciation at herself as she strutted in front of the three-way mirror. She was proud how the pewter- colored silk material clung to her petite frame, and damn if it didn't accentuate the hell out of her ass! And she had much of it to be proud of. It definitely caused quite a commotion in certain circles. Obviously, Denise wasn't alone in her observation, for many compliments were passed her way as she pranced around the bridal salon.

Cyn refused even considering anything that reeked taffeta, 'cause she swore the material was for proms. Denise's demeanor shifted when she heard Vette's big mouth in the front of the salon. She quickly made a beeline for the dressing room and changed back into her two-piece olive green pantsuit.

Unbeknownst to Dee, Vette had spotted her car out in the parking lot, when she initially thought about leaving. But she wasn't having that. She welcomed a chance to take the heat and defend herself if she had to.

Her eyes scanned the salon looking for Denise, who appeared to have disappeared until she saw her coming out of the dressing room.

"Hey, Dee. Our dresses are gorgeous! Did you try yours on yet?" "Don't hey Dee me, bitch! Where did you get off sticking your nose

in Cyn's business? What you did was totally funky! Foul Vette, I don't even know what to say to you," Dee spat out with a vengeance.

"Hold up a minute, don't kick me out of the family yet. The

hardest thing I ever had to do was to tell Cyn about Bashar. I struggled with it for months. I couldn't keep the truth away from her. Enough people had already done that. I wasn't about to be among them," Vette argued. "Oh, you're sorry! That's real convenient! Do you realize that we may be up in here trying on these dresses for nothing if Cyn decides to call off the wedding? Corvette, she is a nervous wreck!'"

Vette hated confrontations and it showed in her face as she became flustered. "Cyn is strong, Denise. She will pull through this with flying colors. Cyndarella is not calling off this wedding, that's not her style."

Denise continued venting, while Vette drew in a deep breath and tried to calm herself. Dee had given her more than she'd bargained for, but she was not taking this lying down. Vette didn't know where her strength came from, but suddenly she heard herself speak.

She had Dee recall the slumber party last month at Cyn's home. Their friend had still believed Bashar had left her at that point, and she wasn't going to let Cyn go on believing something that wasn't true. Besides what kind of friend would she be if she did? Vette was so disturbed by Dee's insinuation that she was hurting Cyndarella she could no longer be in the same room as her. She gave her dress back to the sales clerk and fled from the store. Denise realized she'd been rather hard on Vette, but she couldn't help it. Getting her close friend and business partner down the aisle was the only thing that mattered.

CHAPTER THIRTY-TWO

The last thing Bashar wanted to deal with was his past with Cyndarella Worthy. It was tough enough getting a flight out of San Diego with little notice but he somehow managed, regardless of the cost. He'd surprised his business associates when he called from the airport and told them he was leaving town for a few days. Being the private person that he was, Bashar felt it unnecessary to share the details of his destination. That was nobody's business. A part of him wished Wiyad hadn't told him about her visit from Cyn. Then again, he knew that, as a man, he had an obligation to the woman he'd once loved. She had a right to know what had happened, and it was only fair he faced her in person.

It had been a cold day in January when they'd last seen each other. Bashar remembered lying to his father as they drove to the airport that he'd forgotten his passport. This had angered his dad but it had worked. He'd bought more time to hold Cyndarella once more before he left for Baghdad. Who knew that those ten minutes would turn out to be the best minutes of his life?

On the flight to Detroit, Bashar slept and ate very little. Fortunately, coffee kept him sane. Inside he felt edgy. Life had treated him well since he'd regained his freedom. There wasn't an ounce of lack of confidence in how he felt about himself, especially since he'd made out of captivity alive. If nothing else came out of the time he'd spent isolated, he'd vowed to live life to the fullest in every sense. Up until now, he managed to do just that.

He opened the refrigerator in his hotel room and reached inside for a bottle of Dasani water. Cyndarella, a woman he'd tried hard to forget, still commanded his attention. Time couldn't erase old habits. If Cyn rang the bell, he'd come; she just didn't know it yet.

Wiyad had insisted she should be part of the meeting between Cyn and Bashar, but he'd refused. As relentless as Wiyad was in her approach, Bashar gently reminded his cousin this was something he alone had to do. The family had done more than enough, as far as he was concerned. Wiyad, however, devised a foolproof way of helping Bashar plan a reunion with his former love.

The lavender dress she'd designed for Cyn was complete, and Wiyad arranged a time to have it delivered. Cyn informed Wiyad she'd be working late that evening. Instinctively, Bashar agreed Cyn had to be on her own turf because maybe she would feel less threatened. It had been thirteen years since he had laid eyes on her last. Perhaps seeing her again was a matter of emotional life and death in more ways then he cared to admit.

Bashar's road to recovery after leaving prison had not been a walk in the park. After endless examinations and tests had been done, and had come back negative, he was still confined in a London hospital for post-traumatic stress syndrome and depression. He had severely suffered from both. These disorders were common in former prisoners and hostages. But he made a commitment to beat it. He did it with both in and outpatient treatment, but refusing to take prescription drugs. They were addictive. The medical doctors encouraged him to take them on a short-term basis, but he declined. Back in the day, he had never even smoked a joint, even though his buddies had raved about the stuff.

Gazing at the full size mirror in his suite at the Townsend Hotel, Bashar liked the reflection of the man he witnessed staring back at him. Yes, there wasn't an ounce of lack of confidence in how he felt about himself now. His whole approach to life had taken on a whole new meaning. He would not take anyone in his life for granted. If nothing else came out of the time he'd spent isolated, he'd live life to the fullest in every way. Up until now, he'd managed to do just that.

CHAPTER THIRTY-THREE

"This layout is slamming," Cyn voiced out loud as she reviewed the new designs for the Delectable Diamonds holiday campaign that coincided with the jeweler's thirtieth anniversary. The jeweler wanted to generate traffic by doing something to retain new business and keep the current clientele happy. They'd managed to do it throughout the years without the assistance of an advertising agency, but once they started adding new trading locations, Claud, the owner, had retained Peachtree to handle his business. Cyn had become acquainted with Claud Diamond in her former life as a radio rep, where they'd forged a partnership. Managing his account with great detail had produced enough dollars so that when Cyn left the radio industry, Claud had followed. Glee swelled in Cyn as she continued to review the sample layouts Skip had designed for the Delectable Diamonds holiday campaign. Cyn hoped Wiyad wouldn't keep her waiting. It had been a long day and she was tired.

Sleep was a hard commodity to come by. Cyn was tempted to ask her doctor to prescribe her some of those sleeping pills that were advertised direct to consumers on television and in magazines. Her body was gently showing her signs of fatigue as she yawned repeatedly. Not a poster girl for patience, she quickly approved the sketches for the campaign by signing off on the work order and placed it on Skip's chair, something that had become somewhat of a trademark exchange between the two. If it was in his inbox, it wasn't urgent. However, if it made to the 'hot seat', as it was affectionately nicknamed in the office, it was urgent.

Shutting off the lights in the graphics department, Cyn retreated back to her black leather swivel recliner in her own office for a power nap. A half-hour would do her some good. By the time she woke up, she'd have to use mental boxing gloves to try to pry information out of a reluctant Wiyad. But, first things first, she thought as she drifted off to sleep.

The half-hour nap turned out to be a blessing in disguise. Cyn felt refreshed and, while pouring a glass of Arizona Ice Tea, she heard the after-hours buzzer ring and she paused before heading to the door. She noticed a male figure standing outside her door. She figured he must be lost.

"Can I help you?" she asked through the intercom. She was not prepared for the man's response.

"I was hoping we could help each other, Cyn."

Instantly, Cyn recognized the voice. Stunned, she suddenly felt faint, yet somehow she managed to press the entry buzzer. The well-dressed, serious, handsome man, suited up in black Armani and standing before her, was the eleven-year-old phantom, Bashar Bazzi. Her eyes couldn't focus on his appearance and see how much he'd changed. Shock and rage competed for her attention right now. Any sympathy she thought she'd felt quickly turned into anger as she placed her hand over her mouth in disbelief. Taking a step backwards, her knees buckled, but hurriedly she gained her composure.

"Oh my God, Bashar, you're here. You're really here," she stammered out as she tried to find her voice.

"Yes, Cyndarella. I had to come. It was now or never."

"You selfish bastard!" Before Cyn knew it, her hand had flung a stinging slap across Bashar's face. But before she could strike again, he grabbed her hands. As they wrestled, she tried to wrangle herself free.

"You robbed me of knowing what happened to you! I had every right to know! How dare you?" she lashed out.

Bashar relayed the details of his ordeal to her. When he'd

arrived at Saddam Hussein International Airport with his brothers, they were detained without explanation. Hours later, his brothers were released because they were born in Iraq, unlike Bashar who was born in the nearby country of Jordan. Even though he was American, there was nothing the United States officials could do because Bashar was not a naturalized American citizen. The American Government had cautioned Americans about the possible dangers of traveling abroad due to the growing hostility after the Persian Gulf War, yet they failed to heed the warning.

Bashar looked at how wracked with emotion Cyn was. Even in her distress, she couldn't have looked more exquisite to him than the day they'd first met. The only difference that jumped out at him was the honey-colored highlighted streaks she had in her hair now. He explained he'd been treated in an American Hospital in London for nearly six months after his release because he'd suffered with depression, panic attacks and post-traumatic syndrome after his release. "Being in that hell hole of a prison challenged my soul, and every day I had to fight to save my sanity. I survived, but it took its toll." "Are you okay now?" Cyn asked, genuinely concerned.

"I'm under control, though it took a while, you know, having flashbacks and all. I never knew when an attack would come on. I mean, hearing a plane fly over the hospital would send me into an episode. It reminded me of being held hostage." Bashar's back faced Cyn as he talked and she noticed the slump in his shoulders as he peered outside the window.

CHAPTER THIRTY-FOUR

Bashar looked at the paintings that graced Cyn's office. She still had superior taste. Classic artists like Picasso and the modern Warhol adorned her walls. Bashar noticed a framed picture of Cyn on the cover of *Hour Detroit*, and other newsworthy articles featured prominently throughout the office. A pang of sorrow stabbed at his heart as she reentered the room, handing him a glass of water. Impulsively, he reached for her left hand and noticed her engagement ring.

"Nice rock you got there. When's the big day?" he asked without taking his eyes off hers.

Cyn began to feel uncomfortable, though she didn't know why. "Labor Day weekend."

"That's right around the corner. Congratulations! So who is the lucky man?" he asked, hoping his question didn't seem like an interrogation.

"My fiancé's name is Thad Mitchell. He's truly a wonderful guy. I'm the lucky one," Cyn beamed. Bashar's silence bothered her. Why should he care who she married? she thought to herself. "All right, enough about me. What about you, Mr. Bazzi? How long have you been married?"

Bashar laughed, for Cyn was fishing. He did everything in his power to restrain the joy he felt inside. But he decided he would bait her a little more for fun.

"Why do you assume I'm married? What gives me away?" "Bashar, having a family meant everything to you.

Especially children. I remember that much."

"I remember family was important to both of us. I bet your Thad can't wait to fill the house with kids." The weight of the words caused Cyn to wince. Bashar then indicated that he hadn't married, which dumbfounded her.

"Why not?"

"I've come close with a few relationships. I'm hoping you don't judge me, but I've been around. Traveling, I've met lots of women and I indulged myself. Marriage will happen in time, believe me, I'm not worried." The tension mounted and momentarily both felt uneasy.

BASHAR REGAINED CONTROL again of the conversation. "My family came to visit me after some American diplomats initiated my release. Even though I wasn't in what you'd call the right frame of mind, I thought it was going to be one of the happiest days of my life. Seeing my family again. Seeing you."

"Seeing me?" Cyn's heart raced.

"Why does that seem to surprise you? I thought you knew and perhaps had waited for me." The confession made Cyn's jaw drop as she took in the news. His family then told him she had not been told of his capture which caused him to have an emotional breakdown. After disowning his family, Bashar vowed to go forward and not look back.

"I never came back here. It would have been too hard and I couldn't deal with any more disappointments. I didn't have the right to disrupt your life. I'm glad I didn't. Cyn, look at you! You're doing great, and that's what we always wanted for each other."

"I'm not going to sit here while you feed me a line of bullshit! You're glad you didn't come back? I don't believe you could form your mouth to say something that cruel!"

"Cyn, wait—" Bashar tried to interrupt.

"I've waited a long time for you! But you weren't around to know a damn thing about it, or the misery I went through. I could barely leave our apartment, afraid I would miss an overseas call or a telegram, but instead I got nothing!" A lump formed in Bashar's throat as she finished.

"I held out for months because this was so out of character for you.

I knew something was wrong, but nobody told me," she wept.

Bashar went to Cyn and held her trembling body as she cried. At first, she resisted, then reluctantly gave in to let him hold her. Strong and yet so vulnerable was Bashar's first and only true love. He'd always known that. Even in her pain, to him, she couldn't have appeared anymore lovelier. Her slender face was accentuated by a pair of high cheekbones, and those full lips he longed to kiss. Cyn easily resembled Traci Bingham in the looks department, he noticed, but she was a refined version of the playful actress whom he'd met on several occasions when he'd worked out in California at Billy Blanks' Studio. He gently stroked her hair, soothing her.

"Cyn, you're right, it was selfish of me to assume you'd forgotten about me. But I couldn't blame you after what my family did to both of us. I had to protect myself from the agony of losing you again. In time, maybe you'll forgive me?" he offered.

Shyly Cyn gazed up at the man she once loved. Bashar hadn't changed much. He was still the handsome guy she'd loved a decade ago. His hair was cut shorter now. His physique was rugged and toned.

Unspoken words of affection were perched on the tip of Bashar's tongue. Sensing the heightened strain of emotion engulfing them, he decided to take his leave. As he prepared to go, he knew he had to contain the raw desire surging through his veins. The quicker he got out of Dodge, the better off he'd be.

Cyndarella still got under his skin and she needed consoling. The only way he knew how to comfort her crossed the line.

Pulling out a business card, he wrote down a phone number on the back of it, then he placed in her hands and kissed her on the cheek. Before he could take his leave, she took his hand and stood in front of him, and confessed that she would've waited on him if she'd known the truth. He held her again, this time a bit longer.

He restrained himself, for those eyes and that face he'd adored for a lifetime beckoned him. For both of their sakes, he knew he'd have to tread lightly. Not only did his head betray him, regardless of his good intentions, unfortunately for him, so did his heart.

Distraught with grief, Cyn failed to notice Bashar's slight limp as he walked away.

CHAPTER THIRTY-FIVE

The next morning, Bashar recounted to himself his rendezvous with Cyn. Her revelation that she would have waited had she known what had happened to him had kept him up last night. He chose to ignore the knocks on the locked door from housekeeping to tidy his hotel room. He'd forgotten to put out the Do Not Disturb sign. Seeing Cyn had changed him again. They had been such a part of one another. No other woman would take her place in his life. That was obvious to him now. The bond they shared was just as intense as the love they shared then, and now.

"Cyndarella Worthy loves me," Bashar declared to himself. Cyn hadn't recognized that he walked with a slight limp. For him, that was a good thing. He didn't want her sympathy. Nor did he consider himself in anyway handicapped, either physically or mentally. He had dealt with that part of his life, and also learned how to deal with his issues. He still had trying days, but if things got tough for him to handle, he kept a therapist on retainer. But, for the most part, in recent years, he hadn't needed any

therapy sessions. With any luck, his winning streak would continue.

People spent a lifetime on a search to find a love that would last through all time. Bashar hadn't been one of them. Love had claimed him at the ripe age of sixteen. The cherished memories he had of his past with Cyn had collected dust. He'd willed himself into believing if he stopped reflecting on them, they would go away. But he missed the tiny one bedroom apartment they once occupied. However not every memory was a good one. There was the fighting that mostly stemmed from something family-related.

Chaldean families were a tightknit group that loved a good

party. With the Bazzi clan, they were constant. Cyn chose not to go with him at times. His siblings were cordial to her, but his parents were cold. It made her uncomfortable. He'd threatened them, if they didn't treat her better, he would not attend any of the family functions. Cyn refused to let him miss an event on her account. She'd make him go because she didn't want his family to think she was influencing him otherwise. This scored points with him, but not his parents. The hard part was coming back to their love nest that had turned into a battlefield. Cyn threw a barrage of questions out to him, demanding an answer to each. Once she settled down, he knew it was only temporary.

You couldn't choose the family or tradition you were born into. Bashar was Assyrian. Syriac-speaking Christian people from Iraq and other parts of the Middle East were called Chaldean. The Chaldeans were Eastern-rite Catholics. There was factual documentation detailing how his ancestors were the first people found on earth. People often mistakenly called them Arabs because they were of Middle Eastern descent. The caveat was most Arabs were of Muslim faith, and not Christian, like the Chaldeans. The two shared similarities, particularly, arranged marriages.

The next few days were the busiest of his life. Bashar got in touch with his family to make amends by phone. He wasn't ready to see them in person. Nonetheless, they were glad to hear from him and told him in no uncertain terms that they wanted to see him soon. His mother said she had planned on visiting his aunts and cousins in San Diego within a few weeks. He offered to pay for her airfare. He did visit his father in the nursing home. His mother was grateful, even though his father didn't recognize him.

CHAPTER THIRTY-SIX

Bashar respected Cyn and he wouldn't impede her wedding nuptials if she chose Thad over him. Although Cyn jovially spoke about how wonderful Thad was, she never said she loved him and that intrigued Bashar. Misguided, as it seemed, he remained hopeful. A few hours with her had given him his life back. Once again he felt resurrected. He admired the life she'd built for herself, though frustration seeped into his thoughts as he reminisced on how good things used to be for him too before his life was interrupted.

Bashar had begun watching Cyn in her freshman year. Their first encounter had occurred at basketball practice in the gym. He didn't approach her then because he was shy. He was a year ahead of her, and they continued to cross each other's paths in the hallway or at some of the games but she didn't jock him, unlike most of the other high school girls who did because he was a basketball player.

Bashar proudly wore a gold crucifix necklace around his neck back then. He wore one now. He was a devout Catholic and believed God showed favor upon him the day he initially approached Cyn. It was at that moment, he knew he'd move heaven and earth to get to know her. She was so pretty with her shoulder length hair, bright brown eyes, and a body that every guy on the team lusted after. It was rare that a high school girl would have tits, an ass and legs that would give Tina Turner a run for her money. Yet Cyn had it all and, on top of it, she had fire. And damn, he liked it hot! Little did Cyn know he had gotten an erection from the first exchange of words they'd shared.

Bashar had completed his freshman year at Eastern Michigan University when Cyn graduated from Southfield Lathrup high school. They moved into an off- campus apartment when Bashar decided he would go to school part- time and work in his family's business. Cyn didn't mince words about his decision: she hated the idea. But he did it anyway. The thing that Bashar loved most was coming home and studying together in the evening after dinner. Cyn cooked for him every day except weekends, which didn't matter because they'd dine out together or with friends. Some nights he worked late at the liquor store until it closed, which meant midnight or longer during the summer months. But Cyn would wake up and sit with him while he ate dinner and ask about his day.

Sometimes they'd even watch a video he'd bring home from the store. He'd begged her to stay in bed and get some sleep so she wouldn't be tired at class in the morning, but Cyn didn't hear any of that. He still could hear her saying, "Bazzi, hurry up so we can go to bed." And when they did get to bed..."Ooh, man!" Bashar mouthed with eyes closed and shook his head. If nothing else came to be of this trip, at least he'd have his memories.

CHAPTER THIRTY-SEVEN

The wedding plans were paid in full, relieving Cyn. Thad spent the morning making travel preparations for his daughter, Gia, at the travel agency, where he was also finalizing the details of their honeymoon. Cyn felt a familiar twinge and glanced at the calendar. Her period had come a few days before schedule and that fact frustrated her. What was the purpose of birth control pills if they didn't regulate your cycle? she wondered. Oh well, at least 'Aunt Flo', which she fondly called her period, was paying her a visit. Speaking of which, she searched her purse to find her pill pack to call in a refill when Bashar's card fell out.

"Fuck!" she groaned. She'd struggled with herself endlessly this last week debating whether or not she should phone her former flame. Seeing him had reawakened their connection. It'd also left her exposed. The bad part was Bashar was hip to it. They were both checking each other out. Cyn came to that conclusion before she broke down in his arms. Picking up the phone she called the number written on the card.

"Bashar Bazzi, please."

"May I ask whose calling?" the clerk inquired. This puzzled Cyn.

After all this was a hotel, not his office. "Cyn Worthy."

"Ms. Worthy, Mr. Bazzi requested us to give you a forwarding number."

"Is Mr. Bazzi still a guest at the Townsend?" Cyn questioned.

"I'm sorry, Ms. Worthy, but the only information I have is what was given to you. Is there anything else I can help you with?"

"No thanks." Cyn panicked as she hung up. *Please don't tell me he left again.* She panicked, studying the new number she'd taken down, which had an area code she didn't recognize. She'd kill him if he left town again! The phone rang three times before Bashar answered.

"Hello."

"Don't hello me, where the hell are you? And why didn't you just give me your damn cell phone number instead of sending me on a scavenger hunt? Oh, and by the way, it's Cyn!"

"I recognize your voice very well, Cyndarella. C'mon, now, dear. I thought you'd be intrigued by a little mystery. But if you must know, I'm meeting some business associates in Chicago. Missing me already?" Bashar teased.

"I'm glad you're amused. Are you coming back to Detroit?"
"It depends. Perhaps I will if you ask me nicely."

"Bashar, seriously, you really have to stop this! You're unbelievable! You are so full of yourself ! I would like to see you again before you head back home, and, by the way, you never told me where home was for you."

"You are also full of yourself too! San Diego is where I call home now. And yes to your second question, I'll be back in town Thursday afternoon. Join me for dinner."

Cyn hung up the phone and knew she was in big trouble. Bashar was flirting with her and she enjoyed it. Not to mention how rocked her world was when she thought he'd gone again. Bashar's return sparked a newfound energy that affected her relationship with Thad, who sensed something because she had less time for him, but he backed off, excusing it as wedding jitters. Cyn chose to leave it at that. That didn't mean Thad didn't take it lying down. He sent a dozen of roses to her office, signed, *From a neglected fiancé—guess who?*

Today was Tuesday and Cyn found herself counting the days for Thursday to arrive. Hearing Bashar's voice stirred her juices. This troubled her. The timing for this shit couldn't have been more inopportune. She had to be careful not to motivate Bashar, because he would take the bait. She knew playing with fire was dangerous, but the flames burning inside her couldn't be quenched through sheer will power alone. Cyn considered herself to be very well versed in the Bible. She thought of Adam in the Garden of Eden and, for the first time in her life, she took pity on him. She knew what it felt like to be weak. But unlike Adam, she'd resist her temptation, so help her God. But whom was she kidding?

CHAPTER THIRTY-EIGHT

July was unseasonably hot. Every day in the month ranged in the high nineties, with the heat index factoring in to make it feel like it was 115 degrees outside. Cyn made sure she sported a user-friendly hairstyle that held up in the heat. This summer, she replaced her trademark straight mane for a wavier texture that she could manage without sitting in the salon. All she needed was her Joico styling gel and she was good to go.

Telegraph Road was jammed as she headed north to Franklin Village where her parents lived. She had been so preoccupied these past weeks with her personal drama that she'd kept a cordial distance from her close friends and relatives. She turned into her parents' circular driveway, parked and rang the bell.

"Hey, Cyn, c'mon in. You look very nice," Willa Worthy commented to her appreciative youngest daughter as they shared a quick hug.

"I'm glad I caught you home. Where's Daddy? Ooh, Mother, I know that smell. You baked peach cobbler!" Cyn loved her mother's cooking so much it almost sent her into a jig.

"Your father is in the Florida room catching up on some reading."

The Worthys' home easily could have been featured in *Better Home and Gardens*. Willa had decorated the cozy home tastefully with classic Ethan Allen furnishings throughout. Because of their many travels all over the globe, Cyn's parents had collected rare unique art pieces that highlighted the layout of the sprawling ranch. The Worthys had a knack for entertaining and they did so frequently year-round. Cyn followed her mom like a puppy to the huge kitchen with oak hardwood floors.

"Hey, Daddy!" Cyn embraced her dad. "How's my baby girl?"

"Good, good, good. I'm so glad the wedding plans have been finalized. I can concentrate on other things like moving my things into Thad's and renting my place out." Animation spilled from Cyn's voice, pleasing her parents.

Willa couldn't help but reflect on her children. Having only a son and daughter, the Worthys remained tight. The parents stayed on top of the latest happenings in their kids' lives. Pete had lived in Minneapolis for the last eight years because his wife Julia worked for Northwest Airlines as a Customer Service Manager. Minneapolis was the headquarters for Northwest Airlines, although they did have a major hub in Detroit. Julia had recently put in a transfer to Detroit. The Worthys' son's marriage had seen better days. At the beginning of their relationship, Julia had started out as a flight attendant and was never home. Unfortunately their charming son took advantage of his time alone with other women, which jeopardized his eleven-year marriage.

Now Cyn was ready to stroll down the aisle and nothing pleased Willa and Vernon more. They had become a surrogate family to the majority of their kids' friends, some of whom still remained in their lives from childhood. They were listed in the white pages and received greeting cards when the holidays came around, or an occasional unexpected visit.

The latest pop-in visit left Willa and Vernon standing with their mouths open. Willa enjoyed the closeness Vernon had with his daughter. He told Willa to keep her mouth closed and she promised she'd try, but she couldn't guarantee it. Cyn was fabulous at disguising her emotions. Willa noticed this second wind of energy that radiated from her daughter. Cyn seemed truly committed to Thad, but Willa realized that it was probably a smokescreen.

Vernon witnessed his wife's thought-provoked expression. He

went over to nudge her a bit. At 7 P.M., Willa had a Women's Day meeting at the church and he didn't want her to be late. Besides that, he needed some time to talk to his daughter to let her know she had his support. Vernon saw through her façade. She needed to lighten up a bit and go with the flow.

"Shouldn't you be on your way, dear?" Vernon prodded his wife.

"I am, thank you very much. You're not good at being subtle. Are you trying to get rid of me?" The Worthys' boisterous laughter filled the room.

"My darling, you know better than that. I don't want you running late."

"Mother, do you have to go?" Cyn whined.

"We have a few minutes left, so stop fussing and whining. You know that don't go over well with me!" Willa found her way over to her dining room table and sat down joining Cyn and Vernon.

CHAPTER THIRTY-NINE

"So, when do you go for your final fitting?" "August 2nd." "Remind me, won't you? I want to be there with you, if you don't mind."

Cyn tensed because she *did* mind. She wanted her mother to be just as surprised as the other guests about her dress on her wedding day, but she didn't feel like arguing.

"I'll remind you, Mother."

"Also, the invitations are addressed and stamped. Any last minute changes or anything else you think we need to talk about?"

"Nah, Mom. Nothing I can think of."

"Cyndarella, are you sure? You know I don't like surprises."

"Willa, stop your nonsense," Vernon ordered his wife. He saw where she was headed.

"Mother, what are you talking about?"

"Bashar Bazzi is what *I'm* talking about. When were you going to mention you've been in contact with him?"

Stunned Cyn hung her head for a moment while she gathered herself.

"What about him?"

Vernon saw his daughter struggling and he interrupted before his wife could speak further.

"Baby girl, Bashar came by last week. I got to admit we didn't welcome him with open arms at first, but he changed that.

We know what happened to him Cyn. It was terrible."

"Vernon, it was unspeakable what that young man went through. But life doesn't stop, it goes on. They can't go back. I mean, after all, we are still having a wedding, aren't we?" Willa urged her annoyed daughter for an answer.

"Of course we are. Mother, sometimes you can be impossible." "I'm trying not to be, I'm just concerned. We spent a lot of time and money preparing for this wedding so I have just cause."

"There's really nothing to worry about. I'm handling this fine so you don't have to worry."

"It's okay if you have feelings for him."

"Mother, I've said all there is to say. I'm not getting into this with you. You've got to let me live my own life without you dotting my i's and crossing my t's."

"You're defensive and that says more than enough for me," Willa shot back.

"For God's sake, he was my first love," Cyn exclaimed, exasperated. "But not your last! You are kidding yourself if you think otherwise.

You're betrothed to a man who loves you. Leave Bashar alone or you'll live to regret it, Cyndarella."

"Mother, my feelings for Thad and Bashar are none of your business. It would be so nice if you would stop pushing you're opinions on me and trying to control my life. I don't need it."

It was almost a quarter of seven and Willa had to go now before she was late.

"I'd better be going. Vernon, I'll see you later. Cyn, don't forget what I said. Be satisfied with what you've got, please."

Willa opened the side door leading to the garage and closed the door behind her. Not soon enough as far as Cyn was concerned. Vernon sensed she needed comforting. He knew his daughter had a right to privacy and he gave it to her. Willa, on the other hand, had a mind of her own, like it or not. "Daddy, Mother needs to let me run my life. I don't know how many times I have to say it before it'll sink in."

"You know your mother, Cyn. She's just showing a little concern. Try not to take it personally. So talk to me, Cyn. Just how long have you known about Bashar?"

"A few weeks, really. It seems like a lifetime ago. Vette found out about what happened to him and she thought I should know. Closure, that sort of thing," Cyn offered.

"Vette stumbling onto something doesn't surprise me a bit.

Her timing is off, of course, but how are you handling this?" "Well, Daddy, I practically fainted when I saw Bashar. It seemed like he was watching my every move, it was awkward." Cyn spoke while looking intently at her father, trying to sort out what he was thinking.

"Bashar is sharp, Cyn, always has been, even more so now. He actually wanted to know if he should contact you again before he headed back home or leave you a letter. Apparently you two had a heated discussion. He's a fine man. I've always liked him. I suppose I always will."

"He's in Chicago until Thursday. I agreed to have dinner with him." "Be careful, Cyn. Bashar wears his feelings on his sleeve when it comes to you. He didn't say it, but I think he's still in love with you."

Vernon spoke to his daughter, intuition telling him what might lie ahead but he couldn't afford to delve more than he already had.

"Oh, Dad, I hope not. He deserves someone who'll love him and make him happy, which shouldn't be that hard. He is a remarkable man." Cyn spoke sincerely.

"I get the feeling he has someone in mind to fit the bill," Vernon chuckled.

"Ooh, Daddy, stop that nonsense. But seriously, Daddy, should I tell Thad?"

"Why should you? Cyndarella, there's no harm in having dinner with Bashar. Just as long as that is all you share with him. Just be careful," Vernon warned his daughter. Cyn agreed with her father that she would.

CHAPTER FORTY

Tavie came back into town a week earlier than she anticipated. Mrs. Dooley summoned her to her home to chat. Never fearing she'd have anything to worry about—mainly seeing Mack—Tavie reluctantly agreed. Besides, it wasn't Mrs. Dooley's fault her son had no control over his dick.

Tavie stole a look at herself: her hair had grown out a good three inches. Turning her face side to side, she approved of the new length and decided to grow it out some more and maybe wear a layered flip. She recognized her relationship with Mack was over, no matter how hard he'd pleaded with her. Even unknowingly, the asshole had had a role in the miscarriage of their child. He'd also had the nerve to ask if he could take her to Cyn and Thad's wedding and she'd said, "Hell, no."

Cyn's bridal shower was fast approaching, and when Tavie talked to her friend she was upbeat, happy. She felt hopeful that if Cyn could find love, so could she, and Vette. The latter had begun to panic, but Tavie encouraged her that they were still young and had time. They had a lot to offer a man and didn't have to be desperate. If they acted rashly, payback would be a bitch.

One thing was for certain, Tavie would never date a man longer than one year without an engagement. That was her new rule. All that time she'd given Mack she couldn't get back and he didn't appreciate it. "Lousy son- of-a-bitch!" she fumed.

But she had a new admirer—Orville, the waiter at Jazzman's, who really seemed smitten with her. It would be easy for her to blow off Mrs. Dooley, but she opted not to. She would face the rich, snooty woman and be polite as possible. The only way she'd show off about Orville was if the old bag pushed her.

She wore her favorite outfit for support, a St. John's two-piece Capri pantsuit. Nothing made a woman feel more confident than a favorite outfit. She felt unstoppable as she pulled into the winding driveway of the Dooley's gated Wabeek estate. Once Tavie's presence was known, Mrs. Dooley came out to greet her in the foyer.

"Tavie, you look well," Mrs. Dooley said. "Thanks, Mrs. Dooley."

Mack's mother directed Tavie to come in and sit in the library, a place Tavie use to love. Each bookcase had a theme of books pertaining to art, history, politics, African- American literature, British literature and science. Even mainstream fiction and how-to books had a place, and Tavie had made a point to add a book or two to the collection throughout her courtship with Mack. So much that had gotten her!

Kissing up had gotten her nowhere with Mrs. Dooley, either! She'd only done it to please the man she loved.

Mrs. Dooley had on the lovely two-piece gray lounger Tavie had gotten her for her birthday. "Humph!" Tavie thought to herself. Mrs.

D. was actually trying to be nice. With her freshly coiffed hair wrapped neatly around her stern but nice- looking face, the older woman started in on her.

"Tavie, how have you been this summer, dear?"

"Good. Myrtle Beach was awesome. I struck a seventy before the trip ended. It was quite a treat." Tavie spoke proudly.

"You seem to be very calm and relaxed. I like the way it looks on you. It suits you well. I won't beat around the bush as to why I've invited you here. I'd like very much to help you reconcile with Mack. He's hurting terribly from losing you."

Tavie's mouth fell open upon hearing this. She listened as Mrs. Dooley continued on.

"My goodness, Tavie, I've never seen my son like this and I want to help you both. Is there any room left in your heart for him?" the older woman asked, while her fingers nervously twined around the beaded pearls adorning her neck.

Tavie apprehensively sipped some lemonade before she responded. "Mrs. D., right now, it's the last thing on my mind. I gave Mack everything: my time, love, devotion, and for what? I have to be candid with you, I don't see myself going back to him again."

"I figured as much. That explains his mood. He *does* love you, Tavie.

I'm afraid he didn't realize until it was too late.

I am disappointed. I think you understand him better than the women he's selected in former relationships."

Tavie was visibly shaken by this declaration from Mack's mother. It revealed a side to her that Tavie had failed to unearth throughout her courtship with Mack.

"Mrs. D., thank you. That means a lot to me." She paused, then proceeded, "I'm sorry we didn't have an opportunity to become better acquainted with one another."

"Well, Tavie, my dear, you may not feel the same after you finish hearing me out. I blame the both of you for the breakup of your relationship."

"What? How'd you come up with that one?

"The two of you. My son is quite a catch and you thought the way to keeping him was to shack up with him. But that alone wasn't the downfall, it was your complacency, child!"

Tavie's mouth fell open as she watched Mrs. Dooley hold her shoulders erect and upright as she sat in her Broyhill recliner.

"You're out of line, Mrs. Dooley. I won't sit here and—"

Mrs. Dooley interrupted her. "Dear, that's my point exactly. You *sat* and waited for Mack to make decisions regarding your future together. Sitting is what you did best."

Tavie froze in dismay while hearing the charges being thrown her way.

"Tavie, you allowed yourself to become common. Being a man, he took advantage, and now it's destroying him. My son is now fully aware—he has a conscience as well as a penis!" Mrs. Dooley resounded.

"Mrs. Dooley! I don't know what to say," Tavie muttered. "Tavie, you aren't without fault here. You allowed this crap to mess up your life. I believe you still love my son and if you give it another go, your relationship can be salvaged. It's what solid marriages are made of. Trust me," she finished.

Mrs. Dooley also told her to go out and sow her own oats. Only then could she be sure about where things stood between her and Mack.

"Now, I didn't intend on keeping you here the entire afternoon. We both have things to do, I'm sure." Mrs. Dooley began to rise from her seat, with Tavie joining her.

"Thank you for your insight."

"You're welcome, Tavie. I don't know if your mother ever shared this with you, but make a man thirst for you. Don't give him a glass of water when he knocks at your door. Shucks, give him the pitcher, but only if he's worked hard enough to earn it. Now, I've spoken my mind, and freeing you up to tend to the rest of your day. Where's my hug?"

Tavie retrieved her keys from her purse and approached her ride. Just when she thought she had everything under control. Well, amazingly enough, she agreed with most of the things Mrs. Dooley said. She *had* allowed herself to become complacent in the relationship. The thought of it disgusted her. "Never again," she reasoned with herself. One comment that stuck to her like glue was the one about sowing her wild oats. "Mrs. Dooley, I'm about to do just that."

CHAPTER FORTY-ONE

Vette had spent the past week tidying up her home. It was hard to keep clean when operating a business out of your house.

Gloria Watson, the intake social worker coordinator, had verified most of Vette's references, and she'd also completed the necessary classes the State required to become a foster parent. The reality that so many children were homeless due to the unseen circumstances that their parents inflicted onto them steamed Corvette. Working within the court system, she heard about different cases of child abuse and neglect. Even if she wasn't directly working a case, she'd heard enough from other court reporters, most of whom she'd befriended. She had space available in her home for one, possibly two children, if they were in a sibling situation and didn't want to be separated. She'd go for that.

Vette arose from her futon, which she kept in her basement, and ran upstairs to check her phone messages.

Tavie had apparently made it back from Myrtle Beach and was staying with her aunt in Lathrup Village. Cyn's get- together was the last time when Vette had heard from Tavie and that was back in June, if she wasn't mistaken. Vette wondered why Tavie was calling now. This year, Corvette had learned more about the pitfalls of friendship. The girls and their families had come to her aid and she would never forget that. Holidays were a staple at the Worthys' or the Slades'. It was cool. But Vette would not live in the past if she felt the time had come for her to move on.

With that stunt Denise pulled at the bridal salon, Vette was convinced their friendship would never be quite the same. But Denise had also surprised her. She told her she loved her for always being herself and doing what she felt was right. Dee worried about Cyn because she really wanted her and Thad to make it, and who could fault her for that? Dee had encouraged her to become a foster parent too. She even went to one of the classes with Vette for moral support. Tavie was another story. The women had fences to mend, but Tavie had initiated the first move. Vette decided that some time this week, she would call Tavie and acknowledge her friendship.

The summer winds forcibly blew a strong breeze throughout the large Anderson bay window in Vette's cozy bungalow, making her slightly shiver from their effects. She'd signed up for a couple of online dating services and enjoyed checking out the compatible matches her ad had generated. Being single had advantages if women kept an open mind. Vette was surprised by the number of inquiries she'd received her during the first week. This was definitely comforting. She'd also had an ad in the *Detroit News* personals, which generated a few interesting suitors.

Dialing the 800 line of the dating service, Vette was prompted to enter her password and she was about to do it when her doorbell rang. "Oh crap!" she moaned. She had on old cut-off jean shorts and an oversized Old Navy T-shirt with her pulled back in a ponytail. "I'm not answering it. Maybe they'll go away." But the sound of her doorbell rang out again which sent her to the door.

"Tavie. Hey," Vette greeted her friend. "Are you busy?"

"It's little late for that now, don't you think? Bring your ass in here.

Damn, look at that tan, girlfriend! Even when

I go to the tanning salon, I still don't having it going on like that!" Vette quipped.

"You haven't lost your spunk." Tavie handed over a bag of Sydney Bogg's legendary chocolate covered raisins, along with Alicia Keys' *Unplugged* CD.

"Chocolate covered raisins and Alicia Keys! I love you, boo."

"Cyn would slap you if she heard you with that boo bit! It's been rough but I'm bouncing back."

Vette tilted her head back while directing her attention on Tavie. "Thank you for coming to me about Mack. I listened to his excuses, even though my gut told me different." The pain of raw emotion saturated Tavie's voice as she expressed herself, placing her hand on her forehead. I respect you for telling me, though I needed to believe him. You understand?"

"Girl, absolutely! So stop with that bullshit! We're sisters. Yeah, you infuriated me when you listened to Mack, 'cause I know what I saw."

"I believed you, but I needed to believe in my relationship with Mack too. I mean, I gave some of the best years of my life to that man!"

The women talked through their differences and spent the rest of the afternoon recapturing their friendship. They ended up at Caribou Coffee, sharing lattes and laughter. They promised to never let a man get the better of their relationship again.

CHAPTER FORTY-TWO

Cyn awoke at the crack of dawn on Thursday morning. Thad remained in bed and the alarm went off before he arose. Cyn seemed preoccupied with her morning cup of coffee when he entered the kitchen, placing a kiss on her cheek.

"Good morning, sexy."

"Good morning to you," Cyn said flirtatiously, gazing up at Thad and causing him to blush.

"C'mon now, Cyn, don't look at me like that!" "Like what?" Cyn tried to play dumb.

"Like my ass! Why'd you get up so early, huh?" Thad asked, kissing her.

"Ooh, and what a fine ass it is, sir!" Playfully Cyn grabbed Thad's well-defined gluteus maximus. "Baby, you know I told you Thursday would be a busy day for me. Not only that, we're cutting down on all that bumping and grinding until we're legal."

"Woman, it's been eleven days and counting," Thad fussed. "Hang in there, big fella," she reasoned. Suddenly she started in on an article she'd just read in some women's magazine about fertility. She couldn't wait to conceive their first child.

"I know we agreed we'd start having our baby in March, but I think we should wait."

"Is it because it's in the middle of tax season? We can wait until your workload slows down. Let's postpone our little project until June. How does that sound?" optimistically Cyn asked, making her fiancé squirm.

"Actually I think we should wait at least two years. It would be better for the two of us. I want to have you all to myself as long as I can."

Cyn was incensed by what she heard.

"You expect me to wait two years because you want me all to yourself ? Get real! Oh, that's right, you've been there done that! You weren't planning on disclosing this before we got married, were you?"

"No. I was going to do it before then. Babe, I didn't want to hurt you. C'mon now, don't get started because I haven't been there, done that with you." Thad comfortably reached out to Cyn but she jerked away from his contact.

"Don't you have a shower to take?" she snipped icily.

Thad walked upstairs disappointed, knowing Cyn wouldn't join him. She was devastated. Thad knew what having children meant to her and he'd duped her even before they'd said their 'I dos'. He wanted her all to himself because he'd already had a kid, she convinced herself. It wasn't new to him. That's why she'd refused to be bothered with men who paid child support before, but then she'd relented, made an exception because Thad's daughter, Gia, lived abroad—and now look where it had got her.

CHAPTER FORTY-THREE

"Excuse me, Dee, Wiyad is here in the lobby to see Cyn, and she isn't here yet. You want to speak with her?" The receptionist's voice came through the speakerphone.

"Does she have an appointment with Cyn?" "She didn't say."

"I'll be right there." Denise stood up, pulled down her ivory skirt and walked to the front lobby where Wiyad stood stoically.

"Wiyad! Cyn isn't here, can I help you with something?" Denise offered.

Wiyad shook her head. "Thanks, Denise, but I need to speak with Cyn. It's personal." Wiyad had something on her mind and she wasn't sharing it with Denise, ticking Denise off as she hurried off without saying goodbye.

"Snobby bitch!" Denise muttered to herself as she walked back into her office. She reclined back in her seat and wished Labor Day would hurry up. This *had* to have something to do with Bashar, she concluded. Cyn hadn't mentioned anything about new developments. She appeared to be through with that chapter, which couldn't have pleased Dee more. She pressed the speakerphone button on the phone and starting dialing Cyn's cell phone.

"Yes, Dee."

"Hey, busy lady. Where you at?"

"I'm at Thirteen Mile and Evergreen. I'm pulling in soon. What's up?"

"Wiyad just left here after she came looking for you. She

mentioned leaving you some voicemails," Denise relayed without prying.

"Hmm, wonder what she stopped by for. I wasn't expecting her. I guess I'll call her. Thanks, Dee. See you soon."

Cyn had spent a half morning at her favorite spa getting pampered. Pulling into the Traveler's Tower, she felt compelled to call Wiyad back while out her in her SUV. She wasn't stupid; she knew she had to watch her every move. Denise had become as bad as her mother, which drove her nuts. Absorbed in thought, Cyn jerked when she heard someone call her name. Turning around, she saw Wiyad in her 500 Class Silver Mercedes, beckoning.

"Oh my, Wiyad. I was just about to phone you."

"Cyn, we need to talk. It'll only take a few minutes, I guarantee it." Cyn parked her SUV in the lot as Wiyad waited. Cyn led the woman into the Traveler's Express Cafeteria, where they grabbed a cup of coffee and sat down in the rear. A sigh escaped Wiyad's mouth as she placed a shaky hand over Cyn's.

"Cyn, you're an engaged woman and you're having dinner with Bashar. Why?" she asked.

"He asked," Cyn stated dryly.

"My goodness, you should have said no! This is more than dinner. You must know that."

Carefully, Cyn absorbed Wiyad's words like a sponge. "What are you now? The morality police? Wiyad, there is no harm in it for either of us, and it's really none of your business."

But Wiyad was determined to make her point regardless of Cyn's tone. "Then why aren't you bringing your fiancé to dinner?" she questioned.

"I don't need to. Having dinner with Bashar doesn't make me any less committed to my fiancé."

"Cyn, what I know of you is that you have a good heart and you never lie. Why are you trying to do it now?" Wiyad's line of questioning seemed more like she was accusing Cyn of a crime she hadn't committed. "You have two men whose hearts are on the line, be honest at least about that. My friend, you're transparent. Bashar will see right through you, and trust me when I say that only God can save you when you are uncovered. Good luck, you'll need it." Wiyad swigged the last of her coffee and stood up to leave without regretting a single word she'd exchanged with Cyn. Silently she prayed the other woman would listen.

CHAPTER FORTY-FOUR

The sounds of fax machines, printers and photocopying could be heard through the busy confines of Peachtree Productions. Cyn finished most of the things she had on her agenda. The annual Women in Advertising Conference and awards banquet were being held in Cabo San Lucas in a week. Cyn never missed the event. But because of her upcoming wedding she didn't know whether or not she'd go, or send Denise. A few of the conference members were invited guests to her wedding and they had RSVP'd, according to her mother. That thought propelled Cyn to phone her mom who confirmed everything was basically smooth sailing. Sensing Cyn's lackluster attitude, Willa asked her daughter how things were at her end. Cyn told Willa about her argument with Thad. Her mother agreed Thad should have leveled sooner but they would work things out. They would have to compromise.

Denise knocked and peeked around the slightly open door into Cyn's office, holding files they needed to quickly go over. Cyn signaled to Dee to come in, as she informed her mother she had a meeting she had to tend to. Willa told Cyn to call again when she had a chance, who hung up the phone before her mom had an opportunity to ask about Bashar again.

Subtlety was not an attribute of Denise's. She'd come in on some, but not enough, of the conversation Cyn'd had with Mrs. Worthy. "So, what are you and Thad going to have to compromise on?"

"Damn, you're nosy!" Hearing the annoyance in Cyn's voice, Dee instantly apologized. Cyn could be a bitch when she got into a bad mood.

Cyn told Denise to close the door. "Thad wants us to wait to have children. He didn't tell me until *I* reminded him I was going off the pill in March!"

"Ouch! That is pretty fucked up. How long does he want to wait?" inquisitively Denise asked.

"Two years. Every time I think of it—" Cyn was too steamed to finish her thought.

"Well, it ain't right, but I understand his reasoning. I'm in the same situation. Sean is ready for one more and I'm not. Marla's getting older and Sean's getting very insistent."

"I think we need to plan our fertility clocks. It definitely wouldn't be good business sense if we got knocked up at the same time," Cyn deliberated. The women both were in agreement on that. Cyn resumed their chat. "Dee, if you promised Sean, you should go for it. Besides, think of all the fun you'll having making your new addition!"

Laughter filled the room.

"Okay, it's not a bad idea. Hey, here's a thought. What about a small daycare? We have the space."

"Okay, we'll look into it, and we'll meet on it when I get back from my honeymoon."

Dee rose from her chair, but then remembered the pressing concern she wanted to discuss. "Oh, girl, did you hear Hawthorne Media is going public soon. You know Gunner Hawthorne wants us to be on the same team."

"Yeah, I found out from the main man himself. Gunner's been emailing me. He feels partnering together would make us the largest minority-owned conglomerate in the country!"

CHAPTER FORTY-FIVE

The women separately pondered the subject and surmised it was a huge compliment to be offered such an opportunity. Peachtree's foundation was built on determination and courage, ingredients that were a necessity for success. And, in particular, being a minority business. Cyn used those very tools, along with a combination of experience, education, beauty and quick wit, to lead the agency to the highest level that amazed even her.

Cyn's private line rang: Bashar was on the other end of the phone. Cyn placed him on hold to conclude her business with Denise, who she asked to close the door behind her.

"So, are we still on for dinner?" nonchalantly Cyn asked. "Of course. Meet me at the Jefferson Beach Marina, say between 6:15 and 6:30 at Pier 23. Phone me when you pull into the parking lot and I'll come out and meet you." "Jefferson Beach Marina, why there?" Cyn demanded.

"Please tell me you're not going to kidnap me!"

"I'll explain when you get here. Goodbye for now, Cyndarella." With that, Bashar was gone.

Interstate 94 stayed busy, especially during rush hour. Thad had called before Cyn left home to apologize for their argument this morning. She ignored his calls and refused to listen to the three messages he'd left. She wore an eye- catching striking two-piece Bebe outfit. The nautical top had a plunging neckline. A matching mini skirt accentuated her curvaceous body. She ornamented herself with silver accessories, including hoop earrings and a Gucci link-bracelet watch. Reality set in as she sat in traffic. Suddenly, the realization made her question her decision, but she couldn't turn back now.

Despite everything, she still cared deeply for Bashar, even if they were only friends. If residual feelings lingered, she couldn't bring herself to act on them. She thrived on Thad's love. So what if he got on her damned nerves sometimes! Hell, ain't nobody perfect, herself included, although some days she'd beg to differ. Cyn approached the parking attendant at the booth and he guided her to her destination. She parked, and Bashar came out to get her. She quickly touched up her lipstick and stepped out of her Infinity SUV. Turning around, she locked eyes with Bashar and the moment was electric.

"My God, Cyn. You look incredible!" Bashar never took his eyes off the gorgeous woman standing before him.

"And you look handsome as ever." The two shared a lingering warm embrace that neither of them seemed to want to part from. Bashar directed Cyn inside to an enormous yacht, where the crewmembers helped her aboard. Cheerfully the crewmembers extended a brief tour, upon instruction from Bashar. The yacht was extraordinary. They were led to the upper deck where a table of appetizers and fresh fruit awaited them.

CHAPTER FORTY-SIX

They feasted on seafood and steamed vegetables aboard the rented yacht, sailing down the St. Clair River. Each marveled at the other quietly as they talked of their past. Cyn fought the temptation to glance at Bashar any longer than necessary. Why did he have to look so irresistible? The natural gravitation she felt towards him scared the shit out of her. In a month, she would be Thad's wife, and she would have complete closure if she put Bashar behind her. Sensing the shift in conversation, Bashar decided to change the music in the CD player to something more upbeat before they headed back to the marina.

"Bashar, this is so nice. I didn't expect it."

Touched by her candor, Bashar smiled. "We could've gone to a restaurant, you know," he ventured. Bashar knew Cyn was engaged. People would gossip if they saw the two of them dining in a fine restaurant.

"Gosh, Bazzi, I could have said you were a client."

"Please, woman, the way you look at me gives you away," Bashar expressed amusingly.

"Ooh, you are so wrong. You're the one flirting with me, silly! Though you do look sexy decked out in your Ralph Lauren attire. I mean, you're looking snazzy, Daddy," Cyn said before she could stop herself. "Damn it! I shouldn't have said that! I couldn't help it. You really look handsome. That's the only compliment you'll get from me this evening!"

"I was wondering when you'd acknowledge me by my proper name again. It's been a long time since you called me that. And for the record, I don't think that will be the only compliment I'll receive from you tonight."

"Oh, no, it will be the last one, I can assure you. I really think that you should keep that inflated ego of yours in check. My wit sometimes gets way ahead of me."

"How well do I remember."

The two had crème brulee with fresh berries for dessert. Their waiter, Tom, returned with a bottle of Dom, courtesy of the captain, and opened it for them. After pouring their flutes to the brim, Tom took his leave.

"I'm always amazed by the beauty of sunsets," marveled Cyn.

"I feel the same whenever I look at you." The two exchanged longing knowing glances of desire across the candle lit table with each other. Embarrassed by the intensity of it, Cyn briefly turned away. Soon after, their conversation ensued.

"Hey, so I never found out what you're doing in San Diego. Let me guess; you own a string of 7-11s and gas stations, right?"

"Neither. Now how you like them apples, smart ass! I own several businesses, though I'm a silent partner. Aside from that, I am a hotel broker. I purchase hotels, refurbish them and sell them to the highest bidders all over the world."

"That must be exciting. How'd you end up doing that?" "After I completed therapy, I didn't do anything but travel and meet interesting people from all walks of life. I stumbled into it, actually. I like the lifestyle." "Wow! I'm proud of you!"

"And I you. Peachtree is solid, Cyn, that's great. You deserve the success I hear you're getting."

Cyn relished chronicling the upward mobility of her career, despite her rough stint in the radio industry. Then, you were only good as your rate sheet, which seemed to change by the hour. Basically, she'd allowed herself to be pimped by the local sales managers. Looking back, she believed it was a blessing in disguise. It had given her the determination to do her own thing.

CHAPTER FORTY-SEVEN

Astonishingly, Bashar and Cyn had already polished off two bottles of champagne and it wasn't even 9:00 yet, Cyn noticed, as she looked at her watch. She assumed they would head back early and decided to slow down with the bubbly. There was no way she'd drive while under the influence.

Intently, Bashar studied Cyn's manner. She was more relaxed with each glass of champagne she drank. He had intentionally avoided the subject of her significant other, but that was about to change.

"Tell me about this fiancé of yours."

"Thad, the love of my life, is an accountant. He works for a major firm as an auditor. He does pretty well for himself."

"And the wedding plans?" "Everything is set. We're good to go." "Has he ever been married before?"

Shifting in her chair, Cyn's shoulders stiffened and Bashar noticed he'd struck a chord.

"Not that it's any of your business, but yes. Thad's a divorced father of a precocious child who stays abroad."

"Cyn, you can't be okay with that. For one, you're too jealous and also possessive as hell. You'll be miserable in your marriage. You recognize that, don't you?"

This admission did not digest well with Cyn. "Where do you get off telling me I'm jealous and possessive? That's crazy. I wish you'd stop acting like you know me so well, because obviously you don't!"

Unaffected by Cyn's outburst, Bashar furthered their conversation. "You are territorial, whether you admit it or not. I witnessed it firsthand living with you, remember?"

"You're the one who's jealous as hell because I'm getting married. And as for me being miserable, forget about it."

"Until your stepchild comes for a visit, maybe one longer than you wanted, and intrudes on your time with your husband. You'll be a ticking bomb, poor fella."

"That's fucked up, Bashar, even for you. Maybe I'm wrong for thinking you'd be happy for me. Tell the captain to take us back to the marina," Cyn demanded, throwing her napkin onto the table.

"No, I'm afraid I can't do that. We're too far out now, Cyn. Besides we'll be headed back before eleven. Relax."

"Relax! That's pretty hard for me to do when I'm being insulted!" "I can't take back what I said. You're upset because it's true. I'm having a time imagining you as a stepmother. Some women fit the bill; you don't."

"Oh my God! You're jealous, aren't you? It's still not a reason for you to be a prick!" Cyn spat.

Bashar got up and walked around to Cyn, and held her hands while peering into her brown eyes which glistened with anger. She avoided his stare by focusing her gaze elsewhere. Bashar wasn't deterred by her attitude. Gently, he cupped her face in his hands, forcing her to look at him. He found fault with himself for the hardness that had set inside her.

"Cyn, it's okay, you can talk to me. It breaks my heart to see you so removed from everything. How can I help you? Please tell me. I'll do anything," Bashar pleaded, voice filled with emotion.

CHAPTER FORTY-EIGHT

"Being hard is how I survived. Consumed with grief, Cyn pushed past Bashar and headed to the upper deck where some old school music played. She felt Bashar's hand come to rest on her shoulder as she bit her trembling bottom lip. "You want me to open up? Okay, I will. You're partly responsible for my survival tactics. I mean, it sounds strange, but blaming you helped me get over you. Gosh, I hated you, Bashar." Compelled to expel herself of her demons, Cyn forged on, with a guilt-ridden Bashar hanging on to every single word.

"When you left, I was certain you'd return to me, like you'd promised. But then, the weeks went by, and nothing. Of course your parents were no help to me. I knew it was some kind of conspiracy." Cyn stopped, but Bashar encouraged her to finish.

"I missed you so much. I'd splash on your Caron cologne, and wear one of your T-shirts at night so I could feel close to you again."

"Damn my family! Oh God, how they traumatized you. It's unforgivable."

"I thought you'd had an arranged marriage and moved on," dismally Cyn offered.

"Not on your life! You were going to be *my* wife, remember?"

Silence penetrated the yacht. Cyn and Bashar were consumed with angst. Determined to make the evening eventful, Bashar asked her to dance as an old jam, *The Percolator*, blared through the speakers. They worked up a sweat getting their groove on until Cyn became tired. It was then she noticed Bashar's limp.

"Those monsters hurt you!"

One Foot Outside The Door

The statement perplexed Bashar, but then he realized she referred to his limp. "I'm okay." The pained appearance on Cyn's face concerned him. "I don't want to relive it tonight, Cyn."

Music saturated with Middle Eastern rhythms continued playing and Bashar refused to let her sit down. They continued on when a melodic techno song came on.

He begged for a last dance to a favorite of his.

"Damn, this tune is dope. *Pomegranate* by Trans Global Underground. They're out of London. Since you're so lazy, let me dance for you."

The melodic music played on, enticing Cyn to defy Bashar, much to his enjoyment. She became hypnotized by the combination of the beats. Her moves took on a seductive tone, which were not ignored by Bashar.

"Oh excuse me, my bad! I thought you were too tired to keep up with me."

Enticingly Cyn stepped up to him and playfully reeled him closer to her. Within seconds, she pulled back from the clinch and fled towards the lower deck. Bashar wanted to pursue her but restrained himself. Her agitation caused him to reconsider his actions.

Cyn cursed herself for wanting him. His closeness had got the better of her. She wanted him in a way that was beyond sexual. The light at the end of the storm was

Thad. It had to be! But Bashar's presence jeopardized that fact. And there was nowhere she could hide.

"I've asked the captain to take us back to the marina."

In protest, she shook her head, exasperating him further. "Not yet.

Please, Bazzi. I don't want to leave. I need to be here with you."
"Cyn, what are you saying?"

There would be no more questions, she decided. She was drunk and horny, a risk-taking combination. She acted quickly by unselfishly offering herself to Bashar. The intent of her actions became clear as she stood before him and undressed. "Does this answer your question?"

Bashar whisked Cyn away to a bedroom located on the lower deck of the yacht. The huge, round king-size bed was decorated in rich burgundy and gold colors. Carefully lying her onto the bed, he began disrobing, which fascinated her. Bashar was extremely hairy. Even his back, and often she'd teased him about going to the salon to get it waxed off. But there was no room for laughing now as their passion loomed in the air. Reluctantly Bashar gently asked her if she wanted to halt what seemed to be the inevitable. But she placed a finger over his lips to hush the man she loved. Catching a sight of his underpants caused her to laugh.

"Ah, you're still a boxers man! Are these your favorites?" she mocked.

"I think they're yours."

"Well, what's in them is definitely my favorite."

Their inhibitions disappeared as they began erotically exploring one another. Without missing a beat, Bashar stepped out of his drawers, revealing a well-endowed circumcised cock. The very sight of it turned on an already aroused Cyn more so. Orally she demonstrated how much of an appetite she had for the engorged member inside her mouth, leaving Bashar blissfully moaning her name. Ferociously, she sucked and fucked his cock with her mouth, driving him crazy until he was on the verge of exploding. But that he wasn't about to do. Hell, he'd waited an eternity to have her again.

Taking control, he trailed a highway of love, kissing and caressing every visible part of her body as she writhed in delight. Working towards her clean-shaven pussy, Bashar's tongue lightly traced the outer part of her clit, wooing her. Tenderly he savored her pussy until the sweetness of her juices overflowed in his mouth. He briefly stopped to reach inside the nightstand and pull out a box of condoms, while she quietly took off her engagement ring and placed it beside the bed. She felt somewhat guilty, but she sure as hell wasn't married*now,* and there was no way she'd be bonded by another man's symbol of fidelity as she enjoyed the pleasures of another, anyway.

Condom in place, Cyn climbed on top of Bashar and they began to make love, He switched places with her by positioning her underneath him. Kissing her neck, enticing her more he began to enter her, as her eyes closed in anticipation. The hair on his chest rubbed against her nipples, causing them to become more erect.

"Cyn. Open your eyes." Bashar instructed. "I want you to see your eyes when I enter you, okay, baby? Please!"

Cyn opened her eyes as he commanded and erotically purred as he gradually eased his hardness inside her. Bashar held nothing back, pulling out the stops and captivating her. Over and over again, his hooked-shaped penis dominated her womanhood. His mouth alternated between her full bouncing breasts and lips, causing riveting sensations throughout their bodies, and leading to climax.

Cyn had forgotten how much she loved curling up next to the heat of Bashar's muscular body. She thought the extra insulation made her sleep better. Automatically, she placed her head in the hollow part of Bashar's neck and drifted off; it was a familiar spot, where she'd fallen asleep in the past.

Bashar felt a sense of victory about what had transpired tonight, leaving him too keyed up for sleep. Not only that, there was something comforting about the darkness of the night which made him feel safe, protected. Whatever happened would happen but, right now, tonight was theirs. They'd deal with the consequences in the morning.

CHAPTER FORTY-NINE

Groaning aloud, Cyn awoke to a major hangover. Looking at the empty side of the bed next to her, she wondered where Bashar was. Sitting up, she climbed out of the bed and found her way into the bathroom. Perched on the commode, she urinated to relieve the pressure of her full bladder. After wiping herself, she flushed the toilet and walked over to the sink and washed her hands.

Viewing herself in the mirror, Cyn noticed how flushed her face appeared. Despite feeling like shit and even though her long hair was disheveled, at least she looked good. Reaching below the sink, she searched for toothpaste and an unused toothbrush, which she put to use. Approaching the shower with wobbly legs, she grabbed a fluffy white washcloth and jumped into the shower hoping it would relieve her enormous headache. The citrus scent of the body gel she used invigorated her, while the warmth of the water sprayed upon her achy body.

"Good morning, sleeping beauty. You feeling okay?" Bashar surprised her by entering the shower.

"I'm hung over. Joining me for a scrub?"

A horny Bashar rubbed his hands together in anticipation while they grinned at each other.

"Hell, yeah. You missed a spot." Cyn's well-lathered body, glistening with soapsuds, seemed to beckon Bashar and he responded by reeling her in by the waist against him. Tauntingly, her propped her rear end in his face, was an invitation he couldn't resist. Sliding an index finger up her ass, with slightly bent knees Bashar positioned himself inside her vagina as she trembled like a leaf. Vigorously, he utilized pulsating hip movements, penetrating to a tempo only he and Cyn heard the melody to. Their loving was so lusciously intense it sent chills up and down Cyn's spine, propelling another orgasm. Bashar soon followed suit, and remnants of his love silently went down the drain. Both were oblivious that the crewmembers onboard overheard their lovemaking.

A lively discussion ensued during breakfast, and then silence. Recognizing the view, Cyn observed they were back at Jefferson Beach Marina and suddenly sadness crept in.

"How will Thad take the news?" Bashar questioned. "I don't know."

"You have to tell him."

"No, Bashar, I don't." Agony oozed from her voice.

"Why not, Cyndarella? After last night, for the love of God.

It's me you love!" he insisted.

"Bazzi, I don't remember a time when I haven't loved you. I see that now. But this isn't about you and me."

"You're not making sense. Please help me better understand what the fuck you're saying."

"There's your family, your heritage, the whole Chaldean culture. You can't stay away from them forever. You have to make things right again between you and them. That's why we will never be together. I want no part of it."

"I know why you feel that way, love, I do. My family would love for me to be happy, so they'll accept us. They already have. I mean, let's face it, Cyn, how happy have we've been apart?"

"I'm tired of being strong. I don't have the strength to deal with the drama any more. And there is Thad; I love him too, Bashar."

"Oh, I see now. You prove love for your fiancé by removing

his ring and making love to another man all night long? No man deserves love like that from his fiancée. A slut maybe, but not a wife!" Bashar ranted.

"Bashar, that's low, even for you, don't you think?"

"No, Cyn. What's low is how you're handling this situation." Apparently shaken, Bashar pondered why God would allow his heart to shatter all over again. Taking slow deep breaths, he struggled to calm himself. In the past he'd struggled with panic disorder and the kind of stress he felt could trigger an attack. He retrieved a gift box that he handed to Cyn. Inside was a beautiful perpetual platinum Rolex, encrusted in diamonds.

"Put it on," Bashar directed.

"Oh, Baz, it's exquisite, I can't accept this!"

Ignoring her, he removed the watch from its box and affixed it to her slender wrist.

"Damn straight you can! Consider it an early wedding present. You know, I still recall the time when I first left you." "Oh, Baz. Please don't do this to yourself," Cyn whimpered. "Don't do this! Don't! I can't go back there anymore."

"There's a difference *this* time. When you leave me, I'll own you for life. Remember that! You'll never completely be happy and you know it! You gave me your heart along time ago. I've held it right next to mine and I'll never let it go, as God is my witness." Bashar steadied himself as he was seething from Cyndarella's indecisiveness. He knew that it was best they parted ways now before things took a turn for the worst.

"You will keep this watch as a symbol. When you look at it, recognize that not a minute or second of the day will pass without me loving you. Never, do you hear me? Now, since you're dying to leave, get the hell out of here! Go!" an enraged Bashar roared.

Immediately, a grief-stricken Cyn fled the boat, barely spotting her car and then jumping in. With shaky hands, she started the car as Lara Fabian belted out *Adagio*, courtesy of the CD she had in her player.

Unfortunately every word sent her closer to the edge of despair. Collapsing against the leather steering wheel, her body heaved as she wept in anguish.

CHAPTER FIFTY

Denise decided to pick up a carryout from Sweet Lorraine's and head over to Cyn's for a long lunch. Getting out of the office would give them a chance to really talk. Not that the office hampered that, it was just that both of them were sticklers for keeping Peachtree professional. She picked up a couple of turkey and Swiss cheese sandwiches, fruit salad and Arizona Green Iced Tea. Cyn had got the whole staff hooked on the stuff. Denise touched in the pass code to her friend's gated community and waited for the clearance to proceed.

She noticed a moving company van parked in the driveway as she pulled up beside it. She admired the beautiful landscaping. The rose bushes were full of red and pink blooms, not to mention the gladiolas filling the air with a delicate floral fragrance. Cyn's Hunter Douglas Silhouette Venetian Blinds were open and she spotted her friend admiring her flowers. Invited in, Denise provided Cyn with the bags of lunch and followed her into the kitchen. Cyn told Denise to set everything up while she got an estimate from the movers. Shortly after, she joined Dee for lunch.

"Dee, I'm glad you're here. I've decided to go to the conference." "In Cabo?"

"Precisely. I need a break. It'll be good for me." "Girl, are you still beefing with Thad?"

"Yeah, among other things."

"Among other things, meaning what?"

"Trust me, you don't want to know," Cyn admitted casually, causing Denise to choke on her iced tea.

"Girl, don't make me reach across this table and bitch- slap you. Spill it!"

"Subtlety doesn't become you, does it? Hey, aren't I paying you to get some work done?" Cyn tried to get Dee to back off to no avail.

"I spent the night with Bashar last night." Flippantly Cyn dropped the bomb to an astonished Denise.

"I'm listening, Ms. Worthy. So you gonna tell me what else happened or what?" Dee softly asked her friend, encouraging her to spill the beans. She sat on the edge of her chair not believing what she was hearing. It upset her that Cyn had been sneaking around with Bashar. Cyn painted the picture of the happenings from start to finish, topping it off by showing her the Rolex sparkling on her wrist and the words that had come along with them. Squealing, Dee hated herself for being nosy like this, but this *was* some juicy stuff.

"Let me get this straight. You risked your future for some dick. Was it worth it, Cyn?" The faraway expression on Cyn's face answered Dee's question. "Damn, girl, he put it down on your ass, didn't he?"

"He really did. But it's over and done with now. That's why he is so furious with me."

"This is far from over. You've got yourself into hot water this time, girl. You *have* got to tell Thad."

"Why should I? Men do the same things to us all the time. I'm not telling him a damn thing!"

"Cyn, you have to. I thought you'd gotten over Bashar, but maybe you never have. You've got to level with Thad as soon as possible."

"Get real, Dee, for what? I *still* plan on marrying Thad."

"Yesterday, I might have agreed with you, but now I don't know where in the world you're headed, and neither do you," Dee surmised. "Cyndarella, it really makes me sad."

"Dee, I got this. I'm done with the past now. I assure you my place is with Thad, not Bashar. I'm not dealing with his family again. I told him that. He called me a fucking slut!" Cyn spat out. "Can you believe that shit?"

"I can't believe I'm saying this, but I agree with him totally. I had no idea you had seen, let alone had sex *again*, with Bashar. Cyn, this shit is heavy. Talk to Thad, this cannot wait. I mean, it wouldn't be surprising if Bashar showed up at your wedding under these circumstances. It could get real ugly."

"I hadn't thought of that. I will talk to Thad tonight. Minus some details, of course, for some things are better left unsaid. He won't be happy that I, shall we say, spent time with Bashar, but as long as I not disclose too much information, we'll be fine."

"Hon, you're not the easiest woman in the world to get along with. Bashar could deal with your black ass, keeping you in check and all. You know I would love to see you marry a strong Black brother like Thad, but you might belong with Bashar. If you aren't careful, you could lose them both. That's my two cents for now."

Denise ended lunch with Cyn and headed back to Peachtree. Forgiving someone for cheating was one thing, but how did you forgive someone for loving somebody else? That was a tall order. Denise figured Thad would forgive Cyn her indiscretion. The thing that disturbed her most was Cyn's ambivalence. Cyn needed to admit her feelings and move on with Bashar, but she refused to admit it because she was scared. This latest stunt could cost her the life she'd always dreamt of.

"Perhaps, there may be no happily ever after for Cyn, now or maybe ever," Denise deduced to herself in solace.

CHAPTER FIFTY-ONE

Thad's mood was anything but pleasant. He'd finished auditing a project up in Flint earlier ahead of schedule, but that wasn't surprising for he was real good with beating deadlines. Keeping focused on work helped make time speed along, but it was still difficult concentrating because of the disagreement he'd had with Cyn. The sound of his voice seemed to turn her off, seeing she refused to answer her phone last night.

Thad knew he was solely responsible for her attitude. He should've come clean about planning a family with her. The angry look she'd had on her face weighed on him, because he'd never seen that look before. It was a serious breakdown in their relationship at a critical time; they were significantly sensitive with one another right now because of the wedding.

Thad didn't wish to share Cyn with a child right away, he thought to himself while he smoked a joint. He hadn't toked since the Kappa reunion back in 1997. He'd once been a huge fan of weed, but because his employer random-tested employees for drugs, he'd given it up. Marijuana helped him chill when he was stressed. To him, it was better than taking those antidepressants with side effects like sexual dysfunction. Who needed that?

Everything consumed Cyn, from work, to family, friends and him. That left no room for a baby. Even though she didn't like it, he'd make her see it was right for the two of them temporarily. She'd accused him of feeling that way because of Gia, and that hurt him more than he let on. Gia was his first- born and he loved his daughter. He prayed Cyn would love Gia just as she would the children they'd bore together. Why should this be a competition? Taking off his suit, he went into the bathroom to take a dump and shower, when Cyn arrived and made herself at home.

Establishing herself on the soft camel-colored leather sofa recliner, she was waiting for Thad to come downstairs when she caught whiff of the marijuana. A ceramic ashtray placed on the cocktail table held the remains of the joint, sickening her further. First he led her on about having children, and now he was smoking weed, Cyn stewed, as she heard him approaching.

"Baby, you been here long?" Thad asked kissing Cyn on her lips. "A few minutes. We really need to talk."

Thad winced as she spoke those words. "I messed up, Cyn, I'm sorry. I know you wanted to get pregnant right away, but we need to put it off for at least two years," Thad tried to reason.

"Forget about it. I don't want to have a baby right now anymore.

Dee and Sean are trying, so I'll wait another year."

"That's good for them. Marla needs a brother or sister," Thad stated.

"And what about Gia?"

"Cyn, baby. Please can't we move on?"

"Yes, we can. But what gets me is you knew for months that you didn't want a baby, but you led me on, and damn it, Thad, I'm pissed! And now I come to your home and you're smoking weed? I'm starting to feel like I don't even know you!" "Woman, you're so uptight, maybe you should take a puff or two yourself ! I told you I use to smoke in college. Can't a brother relieve a little stress? I mean, you're sure not trying to give me a little relief. This'll all pass as soon as you get pregnant."

"How do you know you really love me, Thad? You withhold major things from me and expect me to accept it as status quo. It's downright selfish of you and I'm having a hard time dealing with it."

"From the moment we met I knew. We're made for each other; we compliment each other's lifestyle. We go good together. I love you. We're going to have a good life ahead of us. I won't let you down."

"You didn't answer my question. Yeah, we got lots in common but I don't want to be an accompaniment."

Thad's eyebrow rose. "What's that supposed to mean?" "Just that. I don't want to be the cranberry sauce placed next to the turkey and dressing at Thanksgiving time. They go good together too."

Thad's patience with Cyn started to run thin, because she spoke in circles and it was starting to piss him off. With nostrils flaring, he skillfully tried not to let his anger spill over. "What's this shit about turkey and dressing? What's your point?"

"My point is, an accompaniment is replaceable but I'm not. Got it?"

"Hell, baby, I didn't know you were this insecure. All this talk about turkey and dressing...babe, you know I love you."

"So, I completely have your heart?"

"Cyn, didn't I just say I love you?" Thad demanded, when he spotted the pricey watch on an unsuspecting Cyn's wrist.

"Been shopping again, I see." "Not lately, I haven't had time." "How much did you pay for the Rolex?"

Cyn felt her stomach drop to her knees because she'd forgotten to remove the valuable timepiece from her wrist. Only God could help her now.

"It was a gift from a friend."

Thad was not in the mood to be made jealous, but obviously Cyn was trying to pay him back, which angered him. "Must be a good friend. That watch costs thousands of dollars, Cyn."

Her cell phone interrupted the conversation but before she reached it, it'd gone into voicemail. She recognized Bashar's number which made her jumpy.

"Cyn, I'm not in the mood for these games. Tell me how much you dropped on the watch, I won't get mad. You don't have to lie."

"Trust me, I have nothing to lie about. I told you it was a gift. And besides why should you care if I did buy it? I make my own money and I can spend it on anything I want," Cyn snapped.

Thad began pacing back and forth. He knew she was angry with him about not wanting to have children right away, but now she was trying to make him jealous as payback, or so he thought, and it did not resonate well with him.

"I had no idea you'd go these extremes to make me jealous. I don't like it."

"If you're jealous, then that's your problem, not mine," Cyn argued, sending him into a fit of fury. Panic saturated his soul as his body stiffened. Breathing erratically, he recalled Cyn was MIA last night and he started panicking.

Seeing his response prompted her to rush to his side to assist him, but he held up his hand and managed to keep her at bay.

"Cyndarella, so which *friend* did you have dinner with last night? You never did tell me, and obviously you were too busy to answer the phone!"

Cyn knew there was no turning back She had to admit the truth and suffer the consequences. Thad became indignant when he learned that she'd had dinner with Bashar, the 'camel jockey' who'd left her high and dry back in the day.

"Some friend! What did he serve you for dessert? His dick?" Thad barked.

"That's really uncalled for," Cyn challenged.

"Son of a bitch! You fucked that damned camel jockey, didn't you? Answer me! Why are you even here? To tell me it's over and you're kicking me to the curb to marry him, right?"

"No, that's isn't true."

"Goddamned straight you won't! His family will see to that. Cyn, don't let him trick you into thinking otherwise. He's using you like most Chaldean men do Black women. You've been played."

"I should leave."

"So you can go back for more?" Thad hollered. "Whatever lame-assed excuse he gave was good enough for him to hit the skins, regardless of us being *engaged*. What in the fuck were you thinking?" Shaking his head, Thad couldn't comprehend where Cyn's head was based on her actions.

"This is the only time I've cheated on you, and I didn't have to tell you" Cyn offered.

"Ain't that a bitch? Is that supposed to make me feel better? It doesn't. It makes me realize you're not ready to commit, you're too busy being a ho."

"*I'm* not a ho, Thad. I am ready to commit. I made a mistake but I'm not going to keep apologizing for it. Shit, it happened, I said was sorry!" Irritation rose in her voice, infuriating him.

"You have no respect for me or this relationship. Give me my ring back, you selfish, spoiled bitch! You aren't worth the toilet tissue I wipe my ass with!" Thad's words proved lethal, wounding Cyn's self-esteem, though she recovered quickly.

"Careful what you say, motherfucker. In case you forgot, you gave me this!" Cyn rebelled by hurling her engagement ring in his face, before retrieving it and placing it on the fireplace mantle.

Normally she would have continued quarreling but she was whipped from the whole day from start to finish. Thad snatched her key ring and removed his house key.

Exhausted, an emotionless Cyn walked away from his bitter glance without ever witnessing the bitter tears of disappointment streaming down his face.

CHAPTER FIFTY-TWO

A faxed travel itinerary arrived at Cyn's office as she finished her morning meeting with her staff before heading off to Los Cabos. The prominent rock she'd grown accustomed to wearing on her finger was no longer present, but luckily no one seemed to notice, and if they did, they'd not dared to question it. Her attitude was upbeat, not letting on about the conflict she faced in her personal life, though Denise couldn't help but feel her best friend's distress.

Prior to leaving, Cyn had the difficult task of revealing the painful truth about the breakup of her engagement to her parents, crushing them both. Willa offered very little support, acting as if she despised the sight of her only daughter. Three days had passed since she'd heard from either Thad or Bashar. Thad had pretty much said it was over between them. The good thing about this trip was that it would allow her space and time alone to clear her head, something she yearned for. There was hope for her, she told herself, as she boarded the 757 aircraft.

She truly immersed herself in the beauty of the Sol Melia's full-service, Mediterranean style resort at Los Cabos. Nestled away in the Mexican mountains, the upscale five star property blended a cozy ambiance of sunshine and fun with topnotch personal service and the amenities expected of a grand hotel. Mexico held a special place in Cyn's heart. The quaintness of Ixtapa, Cozumel and Puerto Vallarta had lured her back several times with family and friends. Often she relished the old world charm of its cobblestoned streets, elaborate Spanish architecture, kindhearted people and authentic food.

The major wannabe fast food chain restaurants back home didn't hold a candle to a real, traditional Mexican meal.

She couldn't wait to sink her teeth into the food this evening. Registering at the hospitality desk, she received her nametag and a list of the events, including a welcome reception this evening followed by an informal buffet dinner. Running up to her room, she changed into a lime MaxMara linen and rayon dress.

She pulled her hair into a quick bun. She finished with dressing by putting on her gold chandelier earrings. Afterwards, she touched up her makeup, grabbed a small handbag and slipped into a pair of beige Via Spiga leather sandals. She proceeded to the reception area, where conference attendees networked with each other while feasting on scrumptious food and drink. This evening would be a cakewalk compared to tomorrow. There were workshops being held on various subjects pertaining to the empowerment of women in the advertising industry. Cyn had been invited to many private parties that some were having later on in their rooms. She normally avoided settings like that because all it took was one Margarita too many for someone to make a complete idiot of themselves. Politely bowing out, she bid her peers a swift goodnight and retreated to her ocean view suite.

The Women in Leadership seminar scored major points from the women in attendance. The lively interactive discussion revolved around unlimited entrepreneur opportunities to those who were up for the challenge in advertising. Cyn enjoyed the workshop, but emotionally she walked a tightrope, plagued by rampant thoughts of Bashar and Thad that made it impossible for her to focus.

There was a line of hungry folks waiting to grab their grub at the buffet. She couldn't believe the huge selection of goodies displayed: quesadillas, burritos, enchiladas, prepared with cheese, seafood, meat; you name it, it was served.

Cyn wolfed down rock shrimp and lobster enchiladas, along with a side of guacamole. Eating a meal this size so early meant she wouldn't dare attend another workshop this afternoon. There was not a chance in the world she'd be able to concentrate on the lecture now. Well, today clearly wouldn't be a waste, Cyn thought optimistically. Quickly she changed into a swimsuit and headed out to take a nice stroll on the beach. Finding a perfect spot, she laid out on one of the many loungers and fell asleep listening to the sound of waves crashing on the beach.

Segments of her life played out as mini soliloquies refusing to vacate her head. The dialogue was privy to her alone. She recognized love came with its share of baggage. Thing was, you had to decide what amount could you live with. Mothers and fathers played joyfully with their children as she watched forlornly. In that instant, she realized just how lonely she truly was. She grimaced while trying to escape the emotional battle she'd was facing with the two men in her life.

The marketing classes she took in college came in handy. She performed a SWOT—strengths, weaknesses, opportunities, and threats—analysis in the notebook she'd received to take notes during the lectures. Doing an apples- to-apples comparison uncovered Bashar as being a better suitor, based on her results. She wasn't in the least surprised. Her thoughts were of him mostly, and not Thad, for a reason.

CHAPTER FIFTY-THREE

How could any woman forget a man who'd always reminded you how much you were appreciated? Small things like phoning the day after a night a wild lovemaking saying how incredible it was. Bashar had been that man without question. He'd told her she'd be in his thoughts every day. She'd clung onto those cherished memories throughout the years. Other men had paid the price if they treated her less well, which most had. Every woman deserved to have a man love her completely the way Bazzi had loved her at least once in her lifetime. Bashar had given Cyn not only material things, but he'd exposed himself in the purest essence on every single level, even if that had left him vulnerable. However, Bashar had some issues that had caused a rift between them during their relationship. Jealous fits over attention she'd received from other men. And if they'd happened to be Black, Bashar would totally lose his freaking mind!

Dispelling their differences had taken some time. Cyn had insisted they both be honest with each other; if anything made them uncomfortable, they should deal with the issue and not let it fester. Though she wasn't exempt either. She had a jealous streak too, especially when Bashar would attend family weddings and functions without her. Heated arguments had erupted when he left to go to such an occasion. She would remain anxious until he returned home. Cyn thought she had recovered until now.

Although it wasn't a contest between her lovers, she knew Thad loved her dearly in his own way. She dug how proud Thad was of himself and his accomplishments as a successful man. He attacked life with tenacity. She liked that a lot. Showering her with affection had made her blossom— something she hadn't done in a while. However, Thad had some flaws that got on her nerves. Their disagreements stemmed from Thad's know-it-all attitude.

He had to be right. But she didn't back down. He half-heartedly would agree to disagree, saying, 'You can't win em' all'. But the fact he actually wanted to screw afterwards thoroughly disgusted Cyn. He learned fast she wasn't into mechanical fucking. She needed to feel connected.

Family and friends kept commenting on what a fine Black man she had with Thad and it was true, if you were looking at the exterior, though she didn't spend much time thinking much about it. In a way, it seemed like a relief to them that she had chosen to settle down with someone of her own race. After the breakup with Bashar, Cyn remembered her mother telling her to not to ever allow another man of another race make a fool out of her again. It stuck. As did the guilt she experienced in letting everybody down. Within her spirit, calmness touched her soul. She felt an angel had kissed her.

Trying to shed light on the past couple of months, Cyn came to the realization that Thad had started to become possessive of her time. The last thing she needed in her life was another controlling man. Men like that had security issues, and she'd be damned if she would hold Thad's hand throughout their marriage so he could feel okay. And after he dropped the bomb about not wanting to have kids right away even though they'd planned on it, made her doubtful if indeed Thad was the right man for her.

She knew how hard it was to get a business started. She'd struggled the first couple of years getting hers off the ground. When she'd mentioned this to him, he'd seemed to resent her input and did not mince words letting her know about it. Thad should've told her this before they got engaged. If they did get back together, there would be no wedding in the near future. It was clear: they were not ready to say, 'I do'.

IT WAS A WINDY LATE summer afternoon when Willa delivered her beautiful bundle of joy. Willa, though not new to motherhood, found herself overwhelmed when the nurse handed her the latest member of the Worthy family. Wrapped in a soft fleece pink blanket, her newborn baby was breathtaking with rosy cheeks and was fit to be tied. She immediately decided on naming her daughter Cyndarella after the fairytale character. Now, Willa wondered if the name she'd once cherished was the reason for Cyn's behavior.

Willa didn't care what anyone thought of her, but when it came to her children, that was another matter. Peter had his issues dealing with fidelity. However, he had started to mend his ways. But Cyndarella seemed to attract chaos like a moth to a flame, and this time she had been burnt. Thad spoke with Vernon, telling him he was unsure whether he could marry their daughter. Willa understood his logic and empathized with him. She'd had what she called Hot Pants Syndrome back in her day. But she'd also had boundaries and she knew where to draw the line. It was unfathomable to her that Cyn didn't as much as she hated it, Willa couldn't blame Thad one bit. God knew she'd prayed that Thad didn't think Cyn got her morals from her, which disgusted her even more. How in the world could Cyn allow herself to be seduced by another man knowing damn well that she was to be married? Didn't Cyn know there was more to life than a good fuck? Apparently not! Willa tried not to think of Cyn's visit before she took off to Los Cabos, but it haunted the hell out of her. So much so, Willa's blood pressure had elevated to 175/90 for the last few days. Vernon had stayed calm throughout the conversation, yet Willa, being the overly concerned mother, had become unglued.

Willa was proud of how she'd reared her children. Being a librarian had given her access to all kinds of educational books and she'd made sure the children read them. She'd given them reading assignments when school was out and they hated it. But they'd mastered the works of the great poets, like Poe and Thoreau. Literature by Dickens, Hemingway and Shakespeare became some of the children favorites. Like most mothers, Willa wanted nothing for the best for her kids. They lived in a tree-lined subdivision in suburban Detroit and they were considered a part of the upper middle class.

This spring and the summer months had been a happy time filled with wedding plans for her daughter's future but, in one night, she'd thrown it all away for a night of passion. Willa reminded Cyn she wasn't in her twenties anymore and she couldn't go back to the past, no matter how hard she tried; it would never work. Willa could still hear Cyn's reply: "Mother, that's the point; how can I walk away from something I never left?" With that unanswered question left dangling and with a wounded look in her eyes, her child had climbed into the back seat of the limo while the driver had chauffeured her to Detroit Metro Airport.

Willa had a liberal attitude regarding dating outside the color line. She was part Native American. It was evident in her facial features. Many times folks asked what race were she and she proudly told them Black. But she embraced being part Choctaw too. Grandmother shared some native traditional rituals that her family still practiced in her household. She believed in the sanctity of tradition and even had drumming at the birth of both her children. The music had shifted her thoughts away from shooting labor pains. She also had smudging ceremonies with white sage for cleansing the energy in their home.

The Bazzi family had treated Cyndarella like shit. And why? Because she fell in love with their son! Mouna Bazzi made sure not to encourage Cyn by extending a hand of friendship. Willa came close to telling the woman to take her prejudiced ass back to Iraq if she felt her daughter wasn't good enough for Mouna's son. She had to give Bashar credit, though. He had balls and refused to play that game for a long while. He'd stood his ground with his family, and that had made her like and respect him more. At twenty, he'd had courage beyond his years. A man gave up the right to his manhood in Willa's eyes if he was afraid to stand up for his woman. Shit, they might as well call up the plastic surgeon and remove what they obviously did not know how to use.

Sometimes parents had to help their kids clean up their messes, no matter what age they were. Willa tended to Cyn's house while she was away. It dawned on her that Cyn still had a chance to live happily ever after, whether she remained single or got married. Her daughter had worked hard to make a name for herself in the competitive field of advertising where White men ruled. Now, so did Cyn. Being in her daughter's environment somehow healed Willa. The personal effects in Cyn's home showed what hard work and determination could do. The furnishings, from artwork to neutral-toned contemporary furniture, was a sight to behold as Willa walked around the townhouse.

If only Cyn decorated her love life in the same meticulous way she did her home, she wouldn't be knee- deep in this mess, Willa lamented. Not only that, over fifty- five thousand dollars had been shelled out for an upcoming lavish event which Willa was determined not to let go to waste, even if she had to drag Cyn down the aisle kicking and screaming herself. Suddenly, an idea went click in Willa's head as she reclined down on the leopard- print chaise in the den. Slowly a smile appeared on her face and a sense of well being overtook her, something she'd lacked the last couple of days. Faint but recognizable scents of Cyn's perfume filled Willa's nostrils, making her a bit sentimental. "Hold on baby, help is on the way," she choked.

CHAPTER FIFTY-FOUR

It had been days since Bashar had bothered to shower or shave. He'd lacked motivation to leave his house since arriving back to his home in San Diego. Decisively, Cyn had professed her feelings, only to reject him in the same breath, and that had crushed him immensely. Yet, that very thing had made Bashar love her even more, for he understood the rationality. He'd hurt her before, and no matter how valid the reason was, it was too much for her to bear. She was a woman of passion and pain. The reality of this nearly threw Bashar over the edge. Cutting off communication with the outside world this week had helped him deal with the rejection. But he sensed Cyn needed him right now. Somehow he felt her call out to him telepathically and it gnawed at him, because he had resisted the urge to make contact with her. If she wanted a life with him, he'd marry her tomorrow, but she'd have to reach out to him.

Bashar had constant thoughts, remembering the night of love he'd shared with Cyndarella. The unfortunate chain of events that followed saddened him, but he was a survivor. Somehow, their breakup seemed to trigger memories of the time he'd spent in captivity. He recalled befriending many prisoners who never made it out alive. The Iraqi guards would let prisoners' dead bodies rot, and the stench would permeate the air and cause many of the men to puke. A few of his cousins were guards and he received preferential treatment. He was allowed outside in the desert heat, though his feet remained in shackles. The weight of them led to his limp. Always a fighter, Bashar knew he'd make it out in one piece. He just didn't know when.

There were many unanswered questions that he was sure he'd never get the answers to. His father was once a man of great power and highly regarded in Iraq, also in the Chaldean community in the

United States, though on a smaller scale. His father had had to sell some of his family's businesses when he'd left Iraq for America, but he still had a say in how things worked. Bashar knew his father grudgingly accepted Cyn on his account. But he didn't want Bashar to marry her. He was adamant about Bashar following tradition. He wanted his son to ask for the hand of a Chaldean woman in marriage.

"Some tradition!" Bashar debated. In his culture, if a woman wasn't a virgin on her wedding night, the husband had a right to refuse his bride because she was considered damaged goods.

Bashar loved his heritage and sharing it with Cyn, who embraced it. But that wasn't good enough for his father. When talk of Bashar going overseas came up, he went, despite what his gut told him. Something didn't feel quite right about that trip. And he later learned he was right. To this day, he wondered if his father was behind his imprisonment. He found it odd his cousins, who were Iraqi prison guards, always kept him optimistic, which led him to think there was more behind it. But then Saddam had had Bashar's cousins transferred to Fallujah and before they'd left, they told him he'd be home soon. Yet, Bashar would never be able to find out because his father had Alzheimer's now and was in a nursing home.

Bashar hadn't visited any of his family, with the exception of Wiyad, while in Detroit because of the deception. His mother once brought great joy in his life. He knew that it was time to make amends. She loved him and would burst into tears whenever he spoke with her. He needed her right now. Picking up the phone, Bashar reached out to her.

CHAPTER FIFTY-FIVE

Tavie's mind was blown over the whole love triangle thing with Cyn. She learned about the tryst when Dee invited her over. Immediately she grabbed her phone to call Cyn, but Dee told her Cyn was in Los Cabos, which puzzled Tavie. How in the hell could Cyn leave home like this with unfinished business hanging over her head? And Bashar! Where in the hell had *he* come from?

Dee gave her the lowdown on Vette's role in the mix, and Tavie didn't like it one bit. Yet she understood Vette's angle. Vette had given Cyn the facts, and Cyn sought out Bashar. Tavie liked Thad, but that little outburst he'd displayed at the engagement party had been an eye opener. Cyn enjoyed being in the spotlight and so did Thad, something he clearly let be known. He was competitive with Cyn and that was a red flag in Tavie's mind. That was something she'd never had to worry about with Mack. If only he could have kept his dick in his pants, they would still be together.

Amazingly enough, Mack had been relentless in his pursuit of her since the breakup, telling her he was willing to do anything to save their relationship. But Tavie had to remind him they were done. Unlike Cyn, history would not repeat itself again with her and Mack. Heck, she'd lost more than a man, she'd lost her child. Still, there wasn't an ounce of regret inside Tavie. She'd have had to put up with a lot of shit to keep a happy home by overlooking Mack's indiscretions. She would never be able to trust him again. That sobering fact alone kept Tavie from slipping for now.

VETTE GOT HER CUP OF coffee and checked her email. She loved keeping in touch with her friends, for she never knew what kind of silly stuff they'd send her. The little e-cards were cute, but between the pop-up ads and the junk mail, not to mention those dreaded chain letters, going online began to irk Vette. It seemed like half of the personal emails she'd gotten lately had been trash, which she'd kindly deleted without opening them. Scanning through twenty-seven messages, one sender's greeting immediately caught her eye.

Nervously sipping her coffee, Vette's hands trembled as she opened the email. The message concisely written hit home. Cyn didn't blame her! She also apologized for not calling her sooner, and hoped Vette understood and didn't take it personally. Vette knew damn well that Cyn knew she did just that! She was relieved to hear from her friend. She fought with herself over her decision, based on the response she'd gotten from everybody. Mrs. Worthy came through for Vette, which still shocked her. Cyn's mother had told her not to blame herself for being the messenger. Vette believed that had she withheld the vital information from Cyn until after she got married, their friendship would've never been quite right again. Cyn had a right to know.

Vette spotted an Airborne Express truck pulling up out front to deliver a letter, which she signed for. Looking at the address, ripping open the envelope, she prayed its contents would be exactly what she had been waiting for.

DEE MISSED CYN AT THE office. They were more like sisters than friends. Sometimes Dee knew she overstepped her boundaries when it came to the people she loved, and that included Vette. Dee knew she had to smooth things over with her flighty friend. She'd put it off long enough. But she still was angry. If only people could mind their own damn business instead of messing in someone else's, she huffed. Thank God she wasn't in Cyn's shoes! Dee and Sean had developed a close relationship with Thad and, like everyone else, were looking forward to their upcoming nuptial—and now this. Cyn was in way over her head this time, but she was resilient. No doubt she'd bounce back, she had to, even if it meant she ended up flying solo. Dee prayed to God for her friend's sake, that wouldn't be an option.

CHAPTER FIFTY-SIX

Cyn spent the day taking in the sights of Los Cabos. Shopping in the open-air market of Mercado Mexicano was fun. However, bartering for goods seemed to be a necessary evil as the vendors competed for business. She took advantage of some great buys at the Fabrica de Vidrio. Artisans crafted beautiful colorful handblown items from glass. Tourists wandered about salivating over the fine workmanship. The highlight of the afternoon was the glass- bottom boat ride tour out to the arched rocks of Los Arcos where the Sea of Cortes and Pacific Ocean met. The formations were carved by centuries of heavy rain and wind. Amazingly enough, Los Arcos was the only natural preserve within the city of Cabo San Lucas.

Sailing on the catamaran freed Cyn's mind from her troubles back home, as she got caught up in the excitement along with the other women in her group. The food and drinks flowed while animated conversations took place amongst the sightseers onboard. Heading back to the hotel after the boat ride, Cyn was exhausted from all of the day's festivities. A good shower would be good right about now.

After sliding the entry key into the door, she stepped into the spacious sun-filled room. She turned and spotted a huge bouquet of flowers with an attached envelope addressed to her placed on the dresser. Her heart skipped a beat as she held the envelope in her trembling hands. Inside there was contained a formal invitation from Santiago Vela, president of the hotel, requesting her presence for cocktails in the Regal Ballroom at 6:30 P.M. Cyn kicked herself for getting her hopes up thinking either Bashar or Thad would give two shits about her right now. These fancy hotels knew how to pull out the stops to keep you coming back. However, Cyn had decided to take a detour and pass on the invite. She had realized it was time to go home.

If there was a chance she could get a flight out tonight, she would be on it. She knew that she had to move fast, if time was to be on her side, as she dialed the hotel's concierge to assist her. She began to pack her things while waiting on the concierge to call her back with an update. Fortunately the wait was short and, as she was soon to learn, so was her stay. She discovered that she would have to connect through San Diego International and then go on to Detroit. She hated connecting flights, but this itinerary was her only option unless she opted to stay for her originally scheduled flight.

THAD HAD DONE SOME serious soul-searching regarding his future bride. His love for her wasn't in question; it was *her* love for him. He looked back on the weeks prior to her infidelity. She had been distant from him. Thad blamed himself because he didn't want to start a family just yet. The last time they'd made love, it was fine, though she'd quickly pulled away from his embrace afterwards. When he'd reached out for her, she'd claimed it was too hot to snuggle. He left it at that, knowing damn well that he had the central aircon on full blast. He'd figured she was punishing him, but now he realized it was because she had thoughts of Bashar.

Guilt could play tricks with your mind and Thad was not an exception. He wondered if he had relented on having a baby with Cyn, would that would've prevented her from cheating? His heart told him she would not have done it. Heather, his ex-wife, used to tell him that he was selfish, something he'd vehemently denied, until now.

Materialistically, he was generous with the people he loved, but when it came to himself, he had limitations. He liked having his way and could be pretty damn persuasive to make sure he got it. That was one of the reasons that had led to his divorce. And this time, it had cost him the woman he loved.

CHAPTER FIFTY-SEVEN

"You will never know how much I missed every single one of you." Her son had spoken genuinely, and Mouna had sobbed harder when she'd caught sight of him at the London hospital where he was recuperating after his imprisonment. He was clean but appeared very sick. She'd warned Ihklas about the outcome if they didn't bring the girl. She'd even thought of even going to Cyndarella with the truth back then. Ihklas had stopped her.

"Where is she?" Bashar had asked. Where's Cyndarella?" Fear had appeared on their faces as Bashar had become more insistent.

"Mother, where is she?" When he'd requested a phone to call her, her oldest son Faisal had broken the news that Cyndarella would not be joining them. Before her very eyes, Mouna and her family had witnessed Bashar's breakdown, and the nurses had come to escort them away. Bashar had been given a tranquilizer but had asked for them to be banished from the hospital. The psychiatrist on staff had planned on treating him for his ailments both physically and mentally. But now, he suggested the family wait and see which approach was best before contacting Bashar again.

Mouna tried to erase that disturbing encounter. Her mind, however, wasn't in agreement. Neither was Ihklas. Not only did she lose her son that day, she later lost her husband. Several months after, he began to show signs of Alzheimer's disease. Superman had nothing on her husband before the dementia. Ihklas had taken care of their family. She'd married him when she was nineteen and he was thirty-one, twelve years her senior. But those were the good ole days. God finally had his vengeance, Mouna concluded.

The Bazzi family was gathered at an impromptu family

reunion in San Diego. Mouna, the matriarch of the family now, had summoned the five children together which lifted their spirits. They had been estranged from each other for too long and she yearned to have Bashar back in the fold. Bashar was unaware that Wiyad had come to Mouna about his problems with Cyndarella. It was ironic that this same woman, whom they tried to get him to turn away from, was the only one who could return Mouna's son to her and her family. They all loved him dearly, and a part of her died when she'd lost him all those years ago.

Mouna would do whatever it took to keep her family together. Even accepting Cyndarella. She already had. That was the least she could do. She'd done little back in the day to talk her husband out of his scheming to keep the two lovers apart. This had made her an accomplice. The mere thought provoked a feeling of deep shame and embarrassment within her soul. Time had brought upon a change in her. She'd prayed countless prayers to God for forgiveness that would allow old wounds to heal. Mouna attended Mass daily and lit candles for her family. The sins of her past had been forgiven, she convinced herself.

Ikhlas's plan had backfired when his nephews were sent away to oversee another prison in Fallujah. Bashar's imprisonment had turned into a nightmare. There was no way of knowing if Bashar was still alive. Mouna blamed herself and clothed her body in black for a year, something that was common in their culture when a loved one died. She and her husband vowed to take their secret to their graves. It made her sick that Alzheimer's had destroyed her husband's mind, because she knew how delighted he would have been to be reunited with Bashar.

Bashar relayed the full details of his tryst with Cyn to his mother. He begged her not to judge him as he opened up to her and she agreed. Mouna asked him what he wanted from Cyndarella, and he replied that he didn't know. It was then that Mouna took charge.

"How can she know how you feel if you don't know what you want from her, son? No trust, no love."

"I can't imagine my life without her, Mother. Her mom called and told me Cyndarella told her fiancé about us. They called off the wedding. "

"That was courageous of her, my son. I'm sure it wasn't easy. You have your chance now. Your Cyndarella needs to know she can trust you with her life. Then, quickly, marry her!"

Bashar hung his head in frustration. "Mother, I'm not sure she wants to be with me anymore. I said some really mean things to her in the heat of the moment. She hasn't returned my calls."

"Bashar, your anguish is misplaced. You are the source of your own pain. Go to her and make things right. Trust your mother; she won't reject you. Remember the meaning of your name, honey. Bashar means bringer of glad tidings. Now live up to it, my son!" Mouna instructed.

She silently prayed to God for repentance on Bashar's behalf for sleeping with someone's fiancée. The morals of today's young people disturbed her. She found living in the United States a blessing, yet she didn't like some of the sexual freedom that existed there. Sex was for married people. No one could convince her otherwise. The Chaldeans were a proud group of people, yet they'd have to accept Cyn. And, hopefully, she would soon have a new daughter-in-law who would be welcomed by their entire family and community with open arms. Then, the next order of business was she wanted grandchildren. A.S.A.P.

CHAPTER FIFTY-EIGHT

The plane arrived in San Diego, where the rain had started to come down. A short while after landing, Cyn learned that her flight to Detroit was going to be delayed due to the stormy weather. She hated waiting at airports, so much so that she often arrived, just in a nick of time to check in and board. The sight of another magazine stand wasn't nearly as appealing as it had been before the outbound flight to Mexico. She thought of calling her parents or one of her friends, but she didn't want them worrying about her any more than they were already. Besides, it was getting late. She stopped at Jumba Juice to buy a freshly squeezed carrot apple smoothie. It tasted much like the smoothies Bashar used to make for them at breakfast. They'd have smoothies along with a Mediterranean breakfast meat called basturma, which were strips of beef rubbed with red pepper that had been dried slowly in the sun.

"Oh, God, that was so long ago," Cyn sighed to herself. The moment proved to be an epiphany of sorts. It dawned on her she was in San Diego. She reached for her phone and held it in her hand hesitantly. Taking a deep breath, she pressed the speed dial button for Bashar and hoped that he would take her call. He answered immediately when he recognized the caller ID.

"Hello, Cyndarella."

Hearing his voice made her choke back tears. He waited patiently for her to speak. She asked if she was disturbing him and he told her no. He was leaving for a charity dinner to benefit St. Jude's, for children. Danny Thomas founded the charity thirty years ago. And he had always been a big supporter and a long time friend of Marlo Thomas and her family.

"I've been overwhelmed with work. I apologize I haven't

returned your calls. You were right. I was a coward. I got scared. I still am. You've been on my mind and I had to know that you're okay."

It took a moment for Bashar to respond. "I'm fine Cyndarella," he replied drily.

Cyn became discouraged by his aloofness and decided to get straight to the point. "I've been away on a business trip. I have a three-hour layover at San Diego International, and I thought, hell, I don't even know what I thought," she sighed.

"Tell me where you are in the airport."

She provided him with her location and he told her that he was on his way. Cyn went to the nearest bathroom to freshen up, but she was feeling uneasy. Bashar had said little, which was unlike him, and that worried her.

CHAPTER FIFTY-NINE

Bashar got into his car and headed over to the airport. The rain prevented him from driving recklessly; besides, he needed to get to Cyn in one piece. Being a deeply religious man, he felt that God was answering his prayers and he was inspired by his faith. And also by a conversation he'd had with Mrs. Worthy earlier. But he didn't want to get ahead of himself like he did the last time they were together. He would ask her to marry him and if she chose to spend her life with him...The thought alone sent chills down his spine.

He decided to be patient and not let his mind entertain such thoughts. He got Mr. Worthy on the phone and asked for his permission to ask for his daughter's hand in marriage and the older man said yes. Mrs. Worthy wasn't home, and Mr. Worthy told Bashar that he wouldn't tell his wife about the proposal until he heard back from him. He wished Bashar luck. Cyndarella couldn't have asked for a better father. Neither could he.

Pops, the nickname he called the man, had no doubts that he would take care of his daughter.

The fundraiser would have to wait, but his sizeable donation had been taken care of. Mouna was just as excited for her son, that she nearly fainted when he told her Cyndarella was at the airport.

"It's a sign that God is with you!" she wept.

Cyndarella sat inside the airport terminal closest to Delta Airlines on a bench reading *USA Today*. Engrossed in the headlines, she failed to notice Bashar's arrival. When she did, he startled her by kneeling down on his knee, before asking if she would marry him. The proposal blew her away. Bashar grew concerned seeing Cyn so nervous that she couldn't stop shaking. He removed the ring box from his pocket and presented it to her. Instantly she recognized it was from Tiffany's. Her hand trembled as she opened the box which revealed a four-carat emerald-cut platinum and diamond ring.

"Oh, Bazzi, it's beautiful. Yes, I'll marry you!"

Mouna threw together an elaborate celebration for the couple before she headed back to Detroit. Typically, in their religion, a formal engagement party would be held at a banquet hall, followed months later by a shower where presents were presented. Chaldeans gave money to the bride and groom to honor them. She invited the Worthy family, but they declined because they were tending to the details of their daughter's wedding at home. Mouna took time getting to know Cyndarella and found that liking her came easy. The woman was a firecracker, yet, she possessed a kind spirit. The passing years hadn't hurt her in the looks department, either. She could see why her son was smitten with her. It became more apparent through the glances of love they exchanged between one another, making Mouna blush. The party served as the new beginning for the reunited Bazzi family.

CHAPTER SIXTY

Mack had gone out for pastries while Tavie slept. Last night, she'd spent it with him. He needed her. She still needed time. He'd ended his affair with Geneva. The woman had turned into a stalker. He'd had tried to have sex with her again, but his member wouldn't stand up for the occasion. This had never happened to him before. Geneva understood. Her beef was, if he was so in love with Tavie, why did he waste her time? He quickly reminded her, she was responsible for that, not him. Besides, what they shared was based purely on sex.

Tavie awoke and remembered where she was. Mack came in with pastries and coffee. She hoped she hadn't led him on. She still loved him, but she needed someone she could trust forever, not a minute less. Sensing her uneasiness, Mack relayed something personal to put her at ease.

"I'm seeing a therapist. You know, about why I fucked up the way I did."

"What made you take the step?"

"My mother. And you. She said I needed to be honest about my flaws in order for me to be good to someone other than myself."

"Wow, that's pretty amazing. I never thought I'd agree with your mom, but she's right."

"Last night meant everything to me, Tavie. You know we need to get back together, but I won't push it. Just leave the door open."

"That's asking a lot from me. I deserve way better than what you gave me. I'm not going back to that. It won't work."

"Last night we had a breakthrough, Octavia. I'm not messing that up. At some point, if we continue seeing each other, maybe we can try couples' therapy," Mack offered.

Couples' therapy popped again into Tavie's mind as she picked up her bridesmaid's dress. Weddings had a way of making you sentimental, but her foot was firmly affixed on the brake pedal of her frail emotional health. Besides, weddings were a good place to meet new suitors and although Mack would be in attendance as her date, she wouldn't be weak and allow him to disappoint her again.

Cyndarella had made it back home and the Worthys were having a final get together before the wedding rehearsal dinner next week for their friends and family. Tavie had offered Mrs. Worthy her assistance and Willa had taken her, and the rest of the girls, up on it.

Tavie decided she liked her freedom. The quality of men on the dating scene was problematical. She began spending time with Orville, whom she'd thought was just a waiter. Turned out, he was an undercover narcotics agent. Jazzman's was on the up and up, so he was transferred to another restaurant in downtown Birmingham.

Orville considered himself fortunate at being the first Jamaican man she had sex with. He delivered the goods and then some, but he was too needy. She hated that. The sound of his voice, dripping with Caribbean tones, used to turn her on, except when it came to sex.

Orville must have enjoyed the sound of his voice, because he wouldn't shut up. "You like the way this rude boy beat dat face, girl?" he kept inquiring.

Tavie didn't know what the fuck he was saying. He later translated the Jamaican slang. *Beat dat face* meant having sexual intercourse. Tavie was all about sexual healing. Next time she might stick a sock in his mouth when they got it on so it wouldn't happen again. Speaking of the devil, Orville just sent a dirty text message to her on her cell phone. She'd blown him off earlier, saying she wouldn't be available for a few days. But a sister can change her mind, Tavie thought. She decided to stop over for a quickie. The thought of phoning Orville to let him know she was coming over slipped her mind.

Pulling into the Aldinbrooke apartment complex, she made her way to the door. Before she pressed the doorbell, she could hear a conversation through the open window. At the outset, Tavie thought it was the radio or television playing. The laughter coming from the apartment told her otherwise. Orville wasn't alone. Not wanting to be discovered, she decided to break away. There were no strings attached between them. But she froze as she discovered what was going on inside.

"Now I see why Mack is strung out. The bitch knows how to work it out. I wonder how Mack would react to seeing Tavie riding your wood? Orville, good work, you naughty boy!"

"Geneva, stop that. Mack Dooley will never find out. This is for our eyes alone. Besides, you got what you wanted. You're teaching full time in the fall."

"Yes. But in Flint, Orville! Mack hooked me up through an associate there. Though I still have a great deal of desire for him," Geneva said.

"But he rejected you for Tavie."

"He can have her, for now. But if he crosses my path again, he's mine! Truss meh on that. But, right now, ya dun know how much I need you to wash my car," Geneva suggested in their native Jamaican patois.

"Correction, dear. I'm yours, legally speaking anyway. Let me give it to you raggamuffin style, slow like you like it."

Tavie eyes widened in disbelief. She ran back to the car and tried to catch her breath. Orville and Geneva had set her up. They were a dangerous pair. Tavie knew Geneva's last name began with a 'K', because that's what the students called her. It made sense: Geneva and Orville Kirkland were man and wife. And now they had a video of her having sex with him. She would avoid him and tell him she was getting back with Mack. Tavie was sure that would drive home the message she was off limits from now on.

CHAPTER SIXTY-ONE

Denise and Sean received unexpected news. In order for her to get pregnant again, she had to have fibroid tumors removed from her uterus. She'd wondered why she had been bleeding so heavily. The diagnosis explained it. She could get pregnant again within three months of having them removed. The official name of the procedure was called a myomectomy that would leave her uterus intact, according to Dr. Shah, her gynaecologist. The surgery was set for October. Sean told her if she didn't want to have another child, he'd go for adoption. His compassion made her want to give him an army of children. Instead, Dee reassured him that if she didn't have fibroids, she'd have been pregnant by the end of the night.

VETTE COULDN'T CONTAIN her excitement. The wedding was drawing near. Next week, it would be over. Tears brimmed in her eyes as she thought of Cyndarella and Bashar. Orchard Family Services had offered her two children to foster: a brother and sister aged three and four who didn't wish to be separated. She agreed to take them in after the wedding.

The boy was white; his sister was of mixed heritage.

Tara, Vette's mother, told her to freeze her eggs and for the first time in her life, Vette swore at her. It must have done some good because Tara came by with a peace offering. A

$500 Toys R Us gift card and note saying she'd help her arrange the furniture in her house to make it kid-friendly.

Louis provided a much needed shoulder to lean on. His maturity shined while he reviewed the home improvement quotes she'd received to finish her basement. It didn't make sense spending $30,000 if she couldn't get the money back if she tried selling. The area where she lived in Royal Oak had modestly priced homes that had attracted her to the area. But she knew she needed to make a move within a year or so. Louis encouraged her to make it sooner by promising her the down payment on a new house. She had been spending more time at his place, but the kids would change that, though Louis argued it wouldn't. "Let's see what happens with the kids," he'd told her. Unquestionably, she'd wait and see.

THE WORTHYS GAVE A great party for Cyndarella and Bashar, which seemed more like a high school reunion. If tonight were an indicator of how the atmosphere at the upcoming wedding would be, Vette would have to bring tons of tissue. She'd introduced Louis tonight as her boyfriend. Everyone liked him and he fitted right in. Tavie came with her mother, but she managed to tell her about Orville and Geneva. She seemed affected by the sex tape in the duo's possession. Vette talked Tavie into letting it burn for now.

CHAPTER SIXTY-TWO

Family and friends were the biggest losers when a breakup occurred, Thad commiserated with himself. He dropped off Cyndarella's belongings at her parents, where he retrieved his things as well. He couldn't have asked for better-in-laws who might have been. They were great and loved him, more than their own daughter. Cyndarella tried to say goodbye, but he decided it best to deal with her parents. The camel jockey was going to marry her after all. He wasn't one of these men into fronting and saying something just to keep things light. That's why he stayed away from Cyndarella. He didn't want her to be happy; he wanted her to rot in hell.

Thad would truly miss the Worthy family's warmth. He knew he could always count on their support, but the right thing for him to do was move on. As much as he wanted to keep in touch with them, he couldn't. It wasn't good etiquette. In fact, he had listed his home with a realtor. Getting out of Motown as soon as possible was on his agenda. He never wanted to lay eyes on Cyndarella again, not to mention her fiancé. The next time around, he swore he would settle down with a less complex woman who loved him for the man he was, unlike Cyndarella.

CHAPTER SIXTY-THREE

The big day finally arrived. A few minor adjustments were made before the couple exchanged vows. The wedding day had been moved from Saturday to Sunday, which was a popular day for many Chaldean couples to get married. Bashar's family needed the extension for another member of the family to attend. They also changed the location of the reception to the Shenandoah Country Club in West Bloomfield. The final change was Cyn's Vera Wang gown. Wiyad kindly replaced it with a Reem Acra silk gown embellished with elaborate embroideries of three-dimensional flowers that appeared lifelike.

Four-hundred and fifty guests piled in for the nuptials. The sanctuary smelled of sweet roses. Women wearing gorgeous dresses and men in designer suits sat together in the church pews for the candlelit ceremony.

There wasn't a dry eye at Unity Methodist Church as Reverend Ethan Polton married Cyndarella and Bashar. Reverend Polton reminded the couple during the ceremony, marriage was a commitment. Each day together wouldn't be as beautiful as their wedding. They had an obligation now as the keeper of one another's hearts.

"Try not to forget that, you two. God won't," the pastor informed them, before instructing Bashar he could kiss his bride.

CHAPTER SIXTY-FOUR

Bashar stood at the altar in a Joseph Abboud three-button black tuxedo. He reached out and gently lifted the veil of his bride. Within seconds, the two shared a kiss that lingered, until Reverend Polton reminded Bashar to, "Save something for the honeymoon." The onlookers cheered in celebration. The guests headed over to Shenandoah Country Club for a spectacular evening. The band sounded great, Cyndarella thought, as they arrived. She couldn't have conceptualized just how extraordinary the reception room looked. They mingled with guests after dinner, and well-wishers made toasts to the newlyweds.

Cyndarella worried about people might notice her lack of alcohol consumption, but Bashar assured her that no one was paying attention. The two shared a couple of secrets from the attendees. They had already gotten married two days after she accepted his proposal. The ceremony had taken place on a private beach in San Diego. His family's priest from childhood, Father Dally, had married them a week prior to today's ceremony. Adding to this excitement, her period was a no show, delighting them both. They made their way to the dance floor as *Amazed* by Lonestar played. The couple had selected the song for their first dance.

Afterwards, a Grammy award-winning Latino artist made his way to the microphone to serenade the couple. Bashar explained that the musician was a good friend of his and couldn't resist a gratifying love story like theirs. Singing his hit, *The Reason*, brought a thunderous applause from the audience, as everyone began to join the couple on the dance floor.

Willa Worthy finally saw her daughter as the fine woman she'd become. Cyndarella looked like royalty as she and Bashar danced the night away. The tough side of her daughter's personality had dissolved, allowing her to shine like the diamonds that adorned her body. She had come into her own. Mouna interrupted her thoughts by acknowledging how far their children had come, and so had the two families joined by marriage. They were now officially one family.

EPILOGUE

Nadia Alexis Bazzi, made her debut eight months later, weighing in at eight pounds and six ounces. Intense labor pains kicked Cyndarella's ass, but the newborn was worth it. She picked up a substantial amount of weight throughout the pregnancy and was glad most of it had come off after she delivered; however, the extra pounds were stubborn which bothered the new mother. Bashar moved his business from San Diego and sold his home there to his cousin. Cyndarella hired a nanny to assist with the new member of the family when she got ready to go back to work. Not that she had to; Bashar told her she never had to work again. They were financially secure. She decided to work from home, and Denise kept the ship sailing until she returned from maternity leave.

CARLY AND BRENT TOLLIVER, Vette's foster children, blended in well in their new environment. This had been the children's third placement within two years. It was rough at the outset because the children knew nothing about her, other than her name: Ms. Vern. It was like a cat and mouse game discovering who they were. Initially, she was heartbroken to see the children raid the refrigerator at night when they thought she'd turned in for the evening. Immediately, she took charge by informing them they were welcome in her home but they had to follow her rules. Whenever food was served, they could eat all they wanted. After bedtime, they'd have to wait for morning. They understood. She loved them as her own, and so did Louis.

DENISE LIKED THE RESPONSIBILITY of running Peachtree, but she was relieved to know it was temporary. She wasn't as much a people person as she thought. To maintain a successful business, a sense of humor was key. Sometimes Dee got tired of smiling and wanted to curse out some of the associates she dealt with. She didn't like to hold anybody's hand through business deals. Cyn thrived on that. Some of their top clients' heads were so far up Cyn's ass that they treated Dee like a stepchild when Cyn wasn't available. Dr. Shah had given her the green light on getting pregnant, and Sean planned a romantic getaway to Niagara Falls over the Memorial Day weekend. The Falls were considered a good luck charm for creating babies. She'd soon find out for herself.

ORVILLE HAD BEEN UNABLE to contact Tavie. She stopped taking his calls. Perturbed by her behavior, he sent her a text message requesting to see her again. He had been transferred to Saginaw. That got her attention. They met at Jazzman's, where he said he had something to tell her. Tavie astonishingly listened to him tell her about the sex tape they'd made. He told her he lied about erasing it and that his wife caught him watching it. Tavie wanted to know why he never told her he was married, and he replied, "You didn't ask." She realized something about herself in that moment: her communication skills sucked.

Tavie took in the details of Orville and his wife, who had been married three years. They lived apart mostly throughout their short marriage because she was in school in New York working on her degree. A recruiter managed to get him a job right upon graduation at Pace University in law enforcement. Geneva, whom he referred to as 'his wife', never by name, started college later than he had, and so they parted company and saw each other during the holidays. Due to the nature of their relationship, they agreed to an open marriage. As they were leaving, Orville asked Tavie if they could do the nasty again. She said no. It wasn't because of Mack. They still were working through their problems and making progress. Not one to take no for an answer, Orville invited her to at least come and see the Chevy Equinox he'd just purchased because he was tired of driving his company car around on his personal time.

Sean Paul blared inside the incense-filled vehicle, while Orville again found pleasure between Tavie's legs. She knew she should've said no, but his moves were like none she'd ever known. His dark skin and dreadlocks that lightly touched her body as they fucked made her want him more. That wasn't the only reason. She hated Geneva over what she'd lost. Patrons of the restaurant noticed the SUV rocking and assumed it was probably lusty teenagers inside. Geneva picked that time to call Orville, but he was too distracted to answer which Tavie relished. She'd now planned on fucking him in this spot all night long. Revenge was on her mind as she thought of her nemesis. "Payback is a bitch, Geneva, and so am I," Tavie mouthed silently to herself...

Did you love *One Foot Outside The Door*? Then you should read *Betrayal's Dust* by Vina St. Fran!

BOOK 2 OF THE AMOROUS Trilogy: Betrayal, sex and secrets: will the sisters find the happiness they deserve? Cyndarella, Tavie, Denise and Vette have been best friends since junior high, there for each other through the ups, downs, triumphs and tears in their relationships in this sexy, multicultural romance story filled with passion, pain, and everything to gain novel.

ABOUT THE AUTHOR

Vina St. Fran, a confident and vibrant multicultural author, has quickly established herself as a mainstay in the literary world, despite being relatively new on the scene. Best known as the author of the captivating Amorous Trilogy series, she skillfully weaves contemporary romance and erotica romance into her mesmerizing tales, incorporating diverse cultures and perspectives. Ms. St. Fran, a native Michigander, embraces her multicultural background, infusing her stories with rich and vibrant representations of different communities. Residing in the Midwest with her family, she continues to break barriers and provide readers with multicultural narratives that resonate deeply. With her unique storytelling prowess, she captivates audiences from various backgrounds, leaving an indelible mark on the world of romance literature.

www.ingramcontent.com/pod-product-compliance
Lightning Source LLC
Chambersburg PA
CBHW021221260626
47172CB00002B/534